Her Deadly End

Tanya Stone FBI K9 Mystery Thriller

Tikiri Herath

Rebel Diva
ACADEMY PRESS

Her Deadly End

Tanya Stone FBI K9 Mystery Thriller Series

www.TikiriHerath.com

Copyright © Tikiri Herath 2023

Edition: 2023

Library & Archives Canada Cataloging in Publication

E-book ISBN: 978-1-990234-35-4

Paperback ISBN: 978-1-990234-36-1

Hardback ISBN: 978-1-990234-37-8

Audio book ISBN: 978-1-990234-38-5

Large Print ISBN: 978-1-990234-44-6

Author: Tikiri Herath

Publisher Imprint: Rebel Diva Academy Press

Copy Editor: Stephanie Parent

Back Cover Headshot: Aura McKay

Tikiri

A Bonus Gift for You

Here's the secret link to download the twisty bonus epilogue of this book. Learn the surprising turn of events at Paradise Cove a year after the events in this story.

Join my VIP reader club and download your exclusive gift.

Bonus Epilogue: Paradise Cove Twist
https://books.tikiriherath.com/ts-paradisecovetwistsold

◆━━━◆

There is no explicit sex, heavy cursing, or graphic violence in these books. There is, however, a closed circle of suspects, many twists and turns, fast-paced action, and nail-biting suspense.

NO DOG IS EVER HARMED IN THESE BOOKS. But the villains always are.

Tropes you'll find in this mystery thriller series include: female protagonist, women sleuths, detective, police officers, police procedural, crime, murder, kidnapping, missing, creepy cabins, serial killers, dark secrets, small towns, plot twists, shocking endings, revenge, vigilante justice, family lies, intrigue, suspense, and psychological terror.

The Red Heeled Rebels Universe

T he Red Heeled Rebels universe of mystery thrillers, featuring your favorite kick-ass female characters:

◆———◆

Tanya Stone FBI K9 Mystery Thrillers
www.TikiriHerath.com/Thrillers
NEW FBI thriller series starring Tetyana from the Red Heeled Rebels as Special Agent Tanya Stone, and Max, as her loyal German Shepherd. These are serial killer thrillers set in Black Rock, a small upscale resort town on the coast of Washington state.
Her Deadly End
Her Cold Blood
Her Last Lie
Her Secret Crime
Her Perfect Murder

Her Grisly Grave

⋆⊱━━━⊰⋆

Asha Kade Private Detective Murder Mysteries

www.TikiriHerath.com/Mysteries

Each book is a standalone murder mystery thriller, featuring the Red Heeled Rebels, Asha Kade and Katy McCafferty. Asha and Katy receive one million dollars for their favorite children's charity from a secret benefactor's estate every time they solve a cold case.

Merciless Legacy

Merciless Games

Merciless Crimes

Merciless Lies

Merciless Past

Merciless Deaths

⋆⊱━━━⊰⋆

Red Heeled Rebels International Mystery & Crime - The Origin Story

www.TikiriHerath.com/RedHeeledRebels

The award-winning origin story of the Red Heeled Rebels characters. Learn how a rag-tag group of trafficked orphans from different places united to fight for their freedom and their lives, and became a found family.

The Girl Who Crossed the Line

The Girl Who Ran Away

The Girl Who Made Them Pay

The Girl Who Fought to Kill
The Girl Who Broke Free
The Girl Who Knew Their Names
The Girl Who Never Forgot

The Accidental Traveler
www.TikiriHerath.com
An anthology of personal short stories based on the author's sojourns around the world.

The Rebel Diva Nonfiction Series
www.TikiriHerath.com/Nonfiction
Your Rebel Dreams: 6 simple steps to take back control of your life in uncertain times.

Your Rebel Plans: 4 simple steps to getting unstuck and making progress today.

Your Rebel Life: Easy habit hacks to enhance happiness in the 10 key areas of your life.

Bust Your Fears: 3 simple tools to crush your anxieties and squash your stress.

Collaborations
The Boss Chick's Bodacious Destiny Nonfiction Bundle
Dark Shadows 2: Voodoo and Black Magic of New Orleans

Tikiri's novels and nonfiction books are available on all good bookstores around the world.

These books are also available in libraries everywhere. Just ask your friendly local librarian or your local bookstore to order a copy via Ingram Spark.

www.TikiriHerath.com

Happy reading.

HER DEADLY END

AGENT TANYA STONE FBI K9 MYSTERY THRILLER

Chapter One

*I*s someone inside my room?

Eveline Hart blinked and stared into the darkness.

A sense of dread crawled through her body, but she had no idea why.

The backlit clock on the master bedroom wall said it was five thirty in the morning. The windows were shut, and condensation had formed ghostly patterns on the glass. It was still dark outside.

A rustle in the far corner of the room made her freeze.

She wanted to raise her head, but her body had turned to lead. It was like someone had drugged her.

Is this a nightmare? Am I hallucinating? Didn't the doctor say it was going to be rough the first night back?

Her heart thudded like a bass drum.

Did I forget my pills last night?

The rustle came again.

Eveline tried to cry out, but her throat constricted.

A sliver of pale light from the waning moon streamed through the old lace curtains. Her eyes widened as she spotted the shadow in the murky corner by her antique armoire.

The shadow moved.

She glimpsed his face. It had been painted in combat colors. The moonlight fell on a gloved hand and glinted on the sharp edge of a knife.

She gasped in horror.

How did he get in?

Her heart raced. She wanted to scream for help, but no one would hear her. She lived alone in a large house at the end of a cul-de-sac in a quiet neighborhood.

Her phone was on her bed stand, but she lay petrified like a comatose patient, able to hear everything but a prisoner in her body.

Is this how I will die? Raped and murdered in my own bed?

The silhouette moved out of the shadows.

"Where are they?" said a deep voice.

Eveline jerked up with a start.

His voice was muffled, but she recognized it.

So, you came back.

Her stomach lurched.

She now knew why he had painted his face. It gave him sufficient camouflage when he broke into her home, but without a mask, he was making sure she knew who he was.

She knew him all right.

He stepped up to the edge of the bed, the knife pointing at her throat.

"Did you hear me?" he snarled. "You know why I'm here."

Eveline opened her mouth, but no sound came out. He pushed the knife into her neck, drawing a trickle of blood. Every fiber in her body trembled.

"Please don't do this," she whispered. "Please."

He laughed a dry, sardonic laugh—one of a man who knew he held all the cards.

"How could you…?" Eveline's voice cracked.

"I know you took them!" he thundered. "Show me where they are!"

His bellow almost deafened her.

The roar reminded her of her past. A past filled with screaming, hitting, hurting, fighting. Fighting to keep her two sons safe. Fighting to live another day.

She looked into his eyes.

How could you do this to me? Of all people? After all these years?

A coil of fury swirled up her spine, giving her strength and hardening her resolve.

His dark eyes bored into hers. They were like laser beams burning into her heart, but she had made her decision.

She raised her head and steeled herself. "You'll get nothing from me."

The backhanded blow stung. Eveline fell back on her pillow in shock. The throbbing pain pulsated on her cheek.

"You witch!"

He grabbed her by the hair and pulled her out from under the covers.

She tried to push him off, but he was stronger than an ox. Just like his father had been.

He thrust the knife into the soft spot in the middle of her throat. She clasped her hands around his and pulled, but his grip tightened even more.

She gasped for air.

"Get up."

He picked her frail body up by the throat like a puppet master controlling a marionette. He must have known she had just come home from chemotherapy. He must have known she would be too weak to fight.

He shoved her across the bedroom, holding the knife to her neck, one hand crushing her spindly arm so tightly she was sure he'd snap it in two.

He pulled her down the marble staircase. She stumbled, barely registering the pain of banging into the wooden banister.

He dragged her across the living room and threw her into her favorite Empress chair. She spotted the rope lying on the floor.

He came prepared.

Within seconds, he tied her to the chair. Then he leaned in, his angry eyes lit like volcano fire, bubbling and ready to explode.

Eveline was too exhausted to speak, but she knew her time was up.

"If you don't tell me where they are," he growled, his mouth inches from hers, "I'll burn this house down with you in it."

Terror rose inside of her. But it was mixed with a twist of sorrow. She stared back at his soulless eyes, catching a sob in her throat.

You aren't the boy I raised.

Her eyes filled with tears. She closed them as if that would help her unsee the grown man standing in front of her.

You've become your father's son.

Chapter Two

He pulled off his right glove and threw it on the floor.

Eveline instinctively knew what would happen next.

Skin on skin hurt more than that soft wool glove. He'd learned that from his father.

The man cracked his knuckles and clenched his right hand into a fist.

Her eyes grew wide as she noticed the scar on the back of his hand. A glaring red heart burned into his pale skin. The wound had healed, but it was still gruesome.

So, he's been branded too.

"Are you ready to talk?" he roared.

"No."

He slammed his fist into her face. Her head flung back. She reeled. Stars danced in front of her blurred eyes. A metallic taste came to her mouth and blood trickled from her torn lips.

"Don't you want to live, witch?" he shouted, raising his fist, ready to punch again.

She had known this day would come. She just hadn't realized it would be this soon, but she was going to die, anyway. What did she have to lose?

"No."

He hit her again.

And again.

Until she went numb.

With a furious hiss, he kicked the chair violently. It tilted back and crashed to its side, taking Eveline down with it. A searing pain shot through her weakened body like a lightning strike.

Then she blacked out.

She didn't know how long she lay, oblivious to her surroundings.

When she came to, she found herself in a crumpled heap on the floor, still tied to the back of the chair. She lay quietly in that agonizing position, listening to him ransack the house.

"Where are they?" he hollered from somewhere in the dining room.

Something got smashed. The sound of shattering glass came soon after. Her hand-blown wineglasses, the beautiful set she'd bought in Prague, were now gone, she was sure.

She moved her arm and winced at the stinging pain. She felt something strange on her, like a snake had coiled around her.

The rope.

It had loosened when the chair had upturned.

Inch by inch, Eveline pulled at it, ignoring the pains shooting through her body. Soon, the knot came undone, and the rope fell to the floor.

She pushed herself up with shaking arms and glanced around.

A hurricane had passed through the living room. He was upstairs now, cursing loudly.

You'll never find them there.

Eveline got to her feet and leaned against the wall, trying to catch her breath. Her heart was pounding with the effort as much as the terror she felt.

Holding on to the wall, she made her way toward the kitchen. Step by step. She passed the pantry, not daring to glance inside. Instead, she put a trembling hand on the smaller door next to it.

She stepped into the garage and closed the door behind her. Passing her dead husband's Cadillac, she walked toward the Porsche SUV at the end. He used to yell at her for leaving her keys inside, but she only did it because she kept losing them.

Eveline pulled open the driver's side door and crawled inside. She reached toward the cubby-hole and clicked it open. A sigh of relief went through her as she saw her old-fashioned revolver tucked inside.

Her husband had never known she kept it there. If he had found out, he would have confiscated it. She knew it wasn't legal to carry it, especially loaded, but she always felt safer with it.

It took a minute for her to focus.

Foot on brake.

Turn on engine.

Open garage door.

The garage door had pulled up halfway when he came storming through the small door from the kitchen, screaming at the top of his lungs.

"Where the hell do you think you're going?"

Eveline heard the sharp clank of the knife as it hit her back windshield. She jumped on the gas pedal. The Porsche propelled out of the garage, the top scraping the door that was still pulling up.

She rocketed down the driveway and onto the road, grasping the steering wheel like her life depended on it.

She only looked in the rearview mirror once. He was coming. His black pickup truck was gunning out of her driveway, heading in her direction.

She pressed on the gas, glad for her car. She had overheard her husband boast to a friend one day that it had five hundred horsepower or something like that. Whatever it was, she needed everything to beat the heavy-duty flatbed that was coming after her.

Her engine revved as she sped through the quiet streets of Paradise Cove.

She wiped the blood from her face, unsure where she was heading. Her instincts had taken over now and were guiding her toward the town center.

It was still early and most of the town was asleep.

Paradise Cove was a quiet peninsula, inhabited by wealthy retirees and moneyed families who didn't have to get up every day to work. The main street stores were opening, but there was hardly any traffic.

Cora's Corner Café was just a block away. It was where she always picked up her morning latte.

Eveline was no longer thinking. She was on autopilot. She turned the corner, her wheels squealing on the asphalt.

That was when she spotted the boy. She was sure it was him, even with that goofy blonde wig. Her jaw dropped. Her hands clenched.

How did he get out?

That moment of distraction cost her.

One second, she was speeding down the street. The next, she had jumped the curb and was hurtling like a bullet toward Cora's Corner Café.

Day One

Special Agent Tanya Stone

Chapter Three

It's too early for cold-blooded murder.

Tanya Stone gazed out the window of Cora's Corner Café, one hand absentmindedly caressing the sunflower pendant on her neck.

Her Ukrainian-born mother used to tell her sunflowers were a symbol of peace and hope. It was now her good luck charm.

Tanya took a deep breath in. The pleasant aroma of freshly baked buns and chocolate croissants wafted in the air. Asha always knew how to pick the best coffee shops for breakfast.

Seated at a patio table just outside the café doors were her best friends and only family. A slim Asian woman in her early thirties with her long black hair pulled into a ponytail, and an attractive, curvy redhead with bright red lipstick to match her hair. Their heads were bowed, deep in discussion.

Tanya was glad Asha and Katy had wrapped up their most recent cold case. She had been looking forward to spending this week with them, but she wished they'd stop hashing their murder mystery to death.

Didn't they know they were on holiday?

"One dark coffee for you, honey. A Ceylon tea brewed to perfection, and a large chocolate caramel latte with whipped cream for your gal pals."

Tanya turned around to face the café owner.

"That's fifteen dollars," said Cora.

Tanya reached into her cargo pants' pocket, pulled out her wallet, and handed over the cash with a five-dollar tip.

Cora smiled in thanks. "You all new to town, then?"

Tanya nodded.

Cora pushed aside a bag of freshly baked sugar buns and leaned across the counter.

"So, where are you gals from?"

Tanya hated small talk. She hated small talk from strangers even more, but Cora didn't seem to be the type you could ignore and get away from easily.

"Seattle."

"What are you doing in our neck of the woods, honey?"

From the edge of her eyes, Tanya noticed the only other customer in the store, a middle-aged woman with a cane, had stopped browsing the cookies behind the counter and was watching her curiously.

"Just wanted to get away from the hustle for a bit."

"Three lovely ladies like you should be out and about in the big city," said Cora, "shopping, and catching a movie and stuff. There's not much to see in our quiet little town."

"We like quiet."

Cora cocked an eyebrow.

"Anything special you were looking to do in Paradise Cove?"

Tanya gave her a half smile.

Will you stop prying if I tell you I'm an FBI agent? A rookie, but still. And those two ladies outside are my private detective pals.

But Cora was looking up thoughtfully, a finger tapping her chin, as if she was cooking up something.

"There's the sailing club at the end of Sunset Drive. You should ask Hudson Wyatt to take you out on the bay on his yacht this weekend. I think you gals will enjoy it. Tell him I sent you."

"Thanks, but no thanks."

"Well, he's the most eligible bachelor in town and he likes his women tall." Cora winked. "A pretty girl like you should have no trouble finding a date, but he's quite the catch if you're single—"

The bread oven in the back kitchen pinged loudly, distracting her from her nosy inquiries.

Tanya picked up the drink tray and stepped away from the counter before Cora could ask more questions. Just as she reached for the door, a gaunt teenager in a grungy blue hoodie crashed through, almost bowling her over.

"Hey," said Tanya. "Watch it."

The girl brushed past her with a grunt, leaving an unwashed smell behind her.

Shaking her head, Tanya stepped out to the patio to join her friends. She had just handed Asha her tea when they heard the commotion.

"Stop, thief!"

"Someone stop her!"

Tanya jumped up from her chair and spun around.

The teen was scurrying through the door with the bag of sugar buns tucked under her arm. Cora dashed out, yelling.

"Get back here! Thief!"

Tanya leaped off the patio and grabbed the girl by the arm.

"Hey," cried the girl. "Lemme go!"

13

Tanya kept her hold. The kid couldn't have been more than sixteen years old. Her face was scrawny and her arms were so skinny, Tanya could feel her bones.

She was trembling, either out of fear or hunger.

Or both.

"Stop struggling," said Tanya.

The girl's shoulders drooped. She let go of the sugar buns, making the package fall to the ground.

Cora marched over and grabbed the bag. She wagged a furious finger in the girl's face.

"You think you'll get away with this? Just wait till the sheriff hears about what you did. Bad deeds never go unpunished."

"I'll pay for it."

Cora snapped around to Tanya, her chin jutting out.

"What did you say?"

"I'll pay for the buns," said Tanya, still holding on to the girl who'd gone limp. "No need to call the cops. She's just a hungry kid."

A creaky noise made her turn. The woman with the cane was stepping out of the café's front door.

"I phoned Sheriff Reginald," she called out as she limped over to them, her mouth set in a thin, stern line. "He's sending a car over right away."

"Thanks a bunch, Pat." Cora turned back to the girl, who had her head bowed now. "You hear that? The sheriff doesn't like hobos or thieves. He'll throw you in jail. Let's see if you'll try that trick on me again."

"That's enough. I think she got it," said Tanya. "I'm willing to compensate you. I'll pay double for your inconvenience."

Cora turned a stubborn face to her. "Inconvenience? Try living here and see what we have to put up with."

"Let her go, Cora," said a male voice.

Everyone turned.

Tanya stared at the strange man in a tailored blue suit and waistcoat strolling over with a Great Dane on a leash.

Behind him, she spotted a green Jaguar convertible parked on the street, right in front of her Jeep. She had been so caught up with the sugar bun incident, she hadn't noticed the car pull up to the café.

The man looked close to her age, in his early thirties or late twenties—too young to go around dressed up like a nineteenth-century Englishman. His most distinguishing feature was his piercing blue eyes that seemed like they could cut through steel.

Tanya felt a red flag go up.

He might have looked like the most respectable man she'd seen in this town, but something about him was *off*.

Chapter Four

"**G**ood morning to you, Cora."

The suited man walked up to them, shoulders back, arms swinging, and a confident smile on his face.

Tanya sized him up. He was someone important in this town and wanted to make sure everyone knew it.

"There's no need to make a fuss over a bag of buns." He flashed a charming smile at the café owner. "Let the poor kid go."

Cora narrowed her eyes. "Hudson Wyatt, you need to do something about this!"

Tanya raised a brow.

This is the most eligible bachelor of this town?

"The sheriff's team is already on their way," said Cora, crossing her arms. "It's time they started taking these crimes seriously. I'm a small business. I can't afford petty theft."

"You called Sheriff Reginald for *this*? Come on, Cora. I'll pay for the buns if you're that out of pocket."

"Hey," came a voice from behind Tanya. "Would you like some coffee, sweetie?"

Tanya turned to see Katy extending her latte to the homeless girl. "Sit with us."

The girl didn't object to Katy leading her toward their table. She seemed to have given up and accepted her fate.

"You gals better not let her out of your sight," called out Cora. "The sheriff will have strong words if you do."

Tanya went inside the café with Cora, Pat, and the suited man and his dog to settle accounts. She paid for the buns while the man convinced Cora to call the sheriff's office and cancel the complaint.

When Tanya returned to the patio, the girl was seated between her friends, silently sipping the coffee.

"So, do you like the latte, sweetie?" Katy asked her as Tanya took her seat. "Not too sweet for you?"

The girl didn't answer. Her eyes were downcast and her grimy hands clutched the cup like it was the most precious thing in the world.

Tanya pushed the bag of buns toward her with a grin.

"Got you a treat."

The girl didn't speak. She didn't even look up. Her blonde hair dangled over her forehead, but she didn't push it back. It was like she preferred to hide behind her matted locks.

Asha reached over and patted her arm. "You're safe with us. We'll talk to the deputies if they come, okay?"

The girl nodded, and a huge tear dropped on the patio table.

Tanya felt something catch in her throat.

Maybe this is the first time anyone has been decent to her.

But there was something odd about the kid. She had only spoken once when Tanya had wrangled her. Her voice had been deep, like that of a young man, not a teenage girl.

That was when Tanya noticed the Adam's apple. Her eyes passed over the long, scraggly hair. That wasn't real. It was a wig.

The kid's hands were so jittery, the coffee spilled onto the table. Katy picked up a napkin and handed it to her. When the kid reached for it, the sleeve of her hoodie rode up, exposing an ugly red mark of a heart on the back of her hand.

Tanya sat up.

That's not a tattoo. Someone branded the kid. Like they do to cattle.

Who did that?

Asha and Tanya locked eyes across the table. She had noticed it, too.

Asha pulled out her wallet and took out a hundred-dollar bill. She slipped it into the pocket of the kid's torn hoodie.

"For lunch," said Asha with a smile. "Maybe a new hoodie, too."

Katy took a small travel kit from her handbag.

"I have a spare set at home, so you can have this one." She leaned across to the kid and lowered her voice. "It's got a packet of tampons in it, too."

"Er, Katy." Asha gave her friend a warning look. "I don't think..."

"It's okay," said the kid.

Katy pulled back in shock, hearing the deep voice.

"I... I don't need it. Thanks though."

Katy put a hand over her mouth. "I'm sorry. I didn't realize..."

"I dress like a girl because... because they're looking for me."

Asha, Katy, and Tanya exchanged a curious glance.

"Who's looking for you?" said Tanya. "The cops?"

He remained silent, but his right leg was bouncing up and down, a sure sign of nervousness.

"What's your name, hun?" said Asha.

No answer.

Tanya leaned across the table.

"I totally get you. I have a real name I don't use any more either."

The kid looked up, curiosity in his eyes now.

"My real name is Tetyana Shevchenko, but no one can pronounce it. So now, I'm Tanya Stone." Tanya grinned. "I like my new name. What about you? What do you like to call yourself?"

"Jodie."

"How old are you, Jodie?" said Asha.

"Seventeen, I think...," He shrugged. "I dunno."

"There's no need to be scared, Jodie," said Katy. "No one's going to put you in jail for taking bread."

Jodie's face clouded in fear. "But they're going to find me."

"Who?" said Tanya, frowning. "The police?"

Jodie shook his head, and his voice lowered to a whisper. "They'll kill me if they know."

Tanya locked eyes with him. "*Who* will kill—"

An ear-splitting squeal of rubber tires came from the road, cutting her off.

Everyone swiveled around.

A red Porsche SUV was barreling toward them, its engine roaring like an angry dragon. It was aimed at the café's front door.

Tanya's heart raced.

"Watch out!" she shouted, grabbing the kid and Katy, and pulling them to the ground. "Asha, get down!"

They dove from the patio just in time.

The SUV jumped the curb, missing Tanya's Jeep by inches. It crashed into the entrance. The ground shook like a mini earthquake had struck the county.

Shattered glass rained everywhere.

Inside the café, Cora screamed.

Chapter Five

T anya leaped to her feet.

Asha had her phone out and was dialing the emergency number. Katy and the kid were crouched by the bushes, stunned but safe.

Inside the café, the Great Dane barked like mad, and Cora was shrieking like a banshee.

"Wait here," said Tanya.

She jumped over the remnants of the patio and made her way inside.

"Everybody okay?"

Cora was in hysterics by the kitchen door, but otherwise seemed fine. Pat and Wyatt stood paralyzed next to the counter, staring at the Porsche SUV which had most of its nose inside the building.

The vehicle's front bumper had stopped fifteen feet from the counter. The driver was slumped over the steering wheel, partially concealed by the airbags.

In times like these, flashbacks from Tanya's combat days pounded inside her head like machine-gun fire. She shook them off. She had work to do.

The driver was moving. Tanya got closer.

"Hang on. Stay still. We'll get you out soon."

Tanya stepped around the shattered glass and up to the driver's side door.

It was a middle-aged woman with graying hair. Blood was trickling down the side of her face. For some strange reason, she was wearing what looked like a long silk nightgown.

Summoning all her strength, Tanya yanked the door open.

The woman lifted her bloodied head and struggled to get out, but she was still attached to her seat belt. Tanya reached into her pocket for her Swiss Army knife, when the sound of tires squealing came from somewhere in the street.

"Tanya!" That was Asha shouting from outside. She sounded panic stricken. "Get out of the way!"

What's going on?

"Hey!" Asha yelled, banging on the side window now. "Get back! All of you!"

"Another car's coming!" screamed Katy from behind her. "It's going to crash!"

Through the bay window, Tanya spotted the black pickup truck jump the curb, seemingly coming from nowhere.

She spun around. "Get inside the kitchen!" she shouted to Cora, Pat, and Wyatt. *"Now!"*

On the driveway, just outside the demolished entrance, the truck revved.

It's speeding up!

Looks of terror came over Cora and Pat's faces as they realized what was happening. They hurtled into the kitchen, clutching each other. Wyatt dashed after them, pulling his dog's leash so hard, it gagged.

"Tanya!" screeched Katy from outside. "Watch out!"

Tanya jumped over the bakery counter just in time.

The truck rammed into the rear of the SUV. The SUV bucked and slammed into the counter with a thundering crash. Tanya covered her head as wood splinters and wall plaster rained down on her.

Suddenly, the world turned quiet.

It took a few seconds for Tanya to situate herself. The counter had held. She could hear the hiss of the mutilated car engines. She let her arms fall, astounded she was still alive.

A moan came from the SUV.

Tanya got up and looked over the counter to inspect the damage. If the collision had pushed the SUV another ten inches, she would have been crushed to death.

The SUV driver had fallen back on her steering wheel.

Tanya jumped over the counter and tried her door. It was stuck. She banged on the panel and pried it open halfway. Using her knife, she cut the woman's seat belt, but didn't dare to move her.

"You're going to be fine," she said, leaning over the driver to check for broken bones. "EMT is on its way. We'll get you out of here soon."

The woman lifted her head and gave her a glazed look. Her face and shoulders were bleeding.

Tanya put a hand on her arm. "I want you to stay completely still for me, okay? Do not move. That's really important."

The woman gave a hint of a nod.

Tanya turned and trod over to the truck in the back. Its hood was a crumpled mess from the impact, but it wasn't as badly damaged as the Porsche.

The driver, a young male, was staring at the red SUV through his cracked windshield, his eyes dull like a zombie. But it was his face that shocked her. He had painted it green and black, like war paint.

Who is he?

Tanya's brain whirled.

How do two vehicles smash into the same café, minutes after each other?

"Sir?" she called out. "Are you okay?"

He didn't answer, but jerked his head around like he'd just realized where he was. He unbuckled himself and tried the door. It didn't budge.

"Hang tight," called out Tanya. "I'll get you out."

He kicked at the door like a mad bull trying to escape his pen. Tanya yanked the broken door open, expecting to catch him before he fell to the ground.

But he leaped out of the truck. She jumped back in surprise. That was when she noticed the gun in his hand.

"Put that down!" she shouted, but he wasn't listening. He wasn't even looking at her.

Tanya's hand slid to her holster, and she whipped out her bureau-issued Glock.

"I said, lower your weapon."

His glassy eyes stared over her shoulder, his sidearm pointed at the SUV.

"You witch!" he snarled.

"You'll never get them," came a shaky female voice from behind.

Tanya spun around.

The driver of the SUV was hanging out the door, half out of her seat. She looked frail and weak, but in her right hand she clutched an ancient pistol. It was aimed at the man from the pickup truck.

"Lower your weapons!" hollered Tanya, her heart pounding. "Both of you!"

"You're dead, witch!"

Tanya was in their cross hairs.

"Lower your guns! *Now!*"

Tanya saw the man's finger go to the trigger. She dove to the ground. The sound of the gunshot echoed through the air. Inside the kitchen, Cora screamed.

The man crashed to the floor, his face contorted into a horrified expression. His weapon went sliding under his vehicle. A red pool of blood spread around his head.

Tanya jumped to her feet, her heart hammering.

"No!" screamed Asha from outside the window. "Don't do it!"

The woman from the SUV had placed her pistol under her own chin. Tanya sprang forward to snatch the weapon away.

But it was too late.

The woman pulled the trigger.

The bullet rocketed through her skull, killing her instantly.

Chapter Six

"**P**ut your hands up!"

Tanya whirled around.

Asha's call to the emergency services had gone through. A sheriff's deputy stood by the broken door frame, his sidearm out. It was pointed at Tanya.

"Put your weapon on the floor!" he shouted, a sliver of panic in his voice.

Tanya's five-foot-and-eleven-inch frame intimidated most men. She could only imagine what was going through his mind to see her towering over two dead bodies with a sidearm in her hands.

She complied right away.

"Get on the ground!" he yelled.

Tanya lay on her belly, her arms stretched out.

She glanced up as the officer treaded carefully around the wreckage, his eyes wide, and his face green. He looked to be in his early thirties, about her age, but he was reacting like a rookie.

How many murder-suicides would a small, upscale suburb like this have in a decade?

The deputy tugged on his shoulder radio and called for backup. On the floor, Tanya breathed a sigh of relief to hear the sheriff himself was on his way.

She raised her head. "The woman shot the driver of this truck and killed herself." She kept her voice low and calm. "I came inside to help them. I never fired my weapon, Officer."

The cop gawked at her like she was an alien. Tanya squinted at the badge on his lapel.

Blake.

"What do you think you're doing?" came an angry female voice through the busted doorway.

Asha.

"They crashed into the café. Our friend ran in here to save these people, but they pulled their guns on each other."

Katy followed Asha inside, her face red in fury. "She's a good Samaritan!"

Asha marched up to the officer who was standing uncertainly next to the male body, staring at their intrusion.

"Let her go now," said Asha.

Deputy Blake put his arm out. "Get back, ladies. This is a crime scene."

Reaching into the back of his utility belt, he brought out a pair of cuffs. He walked over to Tanya and kneeled next to her. Their eyes met for a second. Without a word, he moved behind her and pulled her arms back before putting the handcuffs on her.

Tanya knew better than to resist. The last thing she needed was to escalate this incident any further.

Cora stepped out of the kitchen.

"Blake?"

The deputy was standing over Tanya, a satisfied expression on his face.

26

"Eveline Hart just shot that man, then killed herself," said Cora, her voice high pitched. "Why are you arresting this girl?"

"Settle down, ma'am," said Blake in a stern voice.

Cora's face darkened. "Don't ma'am me, boy."

"This is a crime scene and I'm in charge."

Pat stumbled out on her cane. "No need to yell. We're rattled enough."

"Geez. I'm not yelling, Aunt Pat. I'm working."

Tanya swiveled her head around toward the café owner.

"Do you know the suicide victim, Cora?"

Cora sniffed. "Eveline never talked to anybody. Kept to herself, but she came here every day for her morning coffee. She lived on Sunset Drive."

"Sunset Drive?" said Katy, looking at her in surprise. "That's where we're staying. At a friend's house."

"Hers is the white one with the gabled roof at the end of the cul-de-sac," said Cora. "It's the biggest house in town, after Hudson's."

Hearing his name, Hudson Wyatt popped his head out of the kitchen door. A horrified expression came over his face as he saw the bodies.

Tanya turned back to Cora. "Is there any reason for Eveline Hart to shoot this man and kill herself?"

Cora shrugged and hugged herself, as if unable to talk anymore. Pat and Wyatt merely stared at the bodies as if they couldn't believe their eyes.

"What about the driver of the pickup?" said Tanya. "Do any of you recognize him?"

The three shook their heads.

"He... he must be from out of town," said Cora.

"Do any of you—"

"That's enough." The deputy gave Tanya an irritated look. "I ask the questions here."

Cora threw her hands up and let out a wail, startling everyone.

"How does something like this even happen? This is a peaceful town!" She let her head fall into her hands. "My bakery's gone. I'm finished. I'm done."

Tanya swiveled around on her stomach to face Cora again.

"Do you have a security camera in here?"

Cora looked up, an annoyed expression on her face. "Of course I do. What do you take me for? I have insurance. I have cameras, but that doesn't help—"

"Cora, please." Tanya raised her head. "Can you get the security footage and show this officer what really happened?"

Cora stared at her and blinked rapidly, like she didn't understand what she had been asked to do. Asha pushed past the cop and stepped over to the kitchen door. She took the café owner by her arm.

"Show me your office."

Tanya watched as Asha led Cora to the back while Katy stood by the window, glowering at the officer, looking like she wanted to whack him.

He was examining the dead woman now, his face scrunched in disgust. He reached toward the revolver next to the SUV.

"Don't touch that!"

He looked up, startled.

"Don't you have gloves?" said Tanya. "That's evidence."

He shot her another irritated glance before pulling a pair out from his belt.

Katy locked eyes with her. Tanya knew what she was thinking. Katy wanted to tell him she was an FBI recruit, but that was not something Tanya wanted to divulge to this rookie.

Who knew how he would react? What if he thought she was lying?

Besides, her FBI badge was inside the Jeep. She had only carried her weapon on her out of habit.

Tanya shook her head briefly. Katy nodded.

Good. She understands.

"The boy?" mouthed Tanya. "Where's the boy?"

Katy whirled around as if she'd just realized they had left the homeless kid behind the broken patio. She peered out of the window, her brow furrowed. Then, she turned back to Tanya and mouthed, "he's gone."

Tanya laid her head back down.

Every nerve in her body screamed at her. *Get on your feet, tell them who you are, and find out why this happened.*

But she wasn't in a position to bargain. Not right now.

Her face was only a few feet away from the blood pooling on the floor. The smell of burned metal and plastic from the mangled vehicles was overpowering. Her head started to throb.

This wasn't how she had planned to launch her FBI career. Her getting arrested, even without justifiable cause, could create a scandal at headquarters. She could lose her job.

Or worse, get imprisoned.

For double homicide.

Chapter Seven

A sha came out of the kitchen with a laptop.

Cora trailed behind her, wringing her hands, her eyes lined with anxiety.

Pat was standing by the kitchen door, leaning on her cane. Wyatt was next to her with the Great Dane by his feet. The dog eyed Tanya with doleful eyes.

Asha dropped the laptop on the counter and turned the screen to face the deputy.

"Officer? You need to see this."

Deputy Blake jumped to his feet. He stepped toward the counter, his eyes widening as the video played.

Tanya turned her attention to the dead woman by the Porsche. She looked like she had been in her sixties. She was wearing an expensive nightgown with the initials *EH* embroidered on the lapel.

EH for Eveline Hart.

Her dress meant Eveline hadn't planned this mad rampage. She had woken up in her home, then somehow got involved with the man she just shot.

But why did she commit suicide?

Tanya turned her head to examine the murder victim lying in a pool of blood next to his truck.

He was much younger, in this mid-twenties or thereabouts. He was dressed in all black. His pants, T-shirt, jacket, and cap looked like what a stereotypical bank robber would wear. He had one glove on his left hand, but his right hand was bare.

But it was his painted face that puzzled her.

If he had wanted to dress for camouflage, why hadn't he used a balaclava or a ski mask?

She stared at him, trying to think of various scenarios where two vehicles would crash into a café one after the other. The truck had to have been chasing the SUV. But one thing she could say for sure. The woman in the SUV had been a good shot. The bullet had gone straight in between his eyes.

Eveline Hart wouldn't have fired at him and killed herself, if they hadn't had a relationship—a tumultuous one that would end in murder-suicide. But she looked old enough to be his mother.

Her brain whirred.

What was their connection?

Tanya scanned the man's body. She had seen the airbags deploy in the truck, which would account for the bruises on his face. But it was his hand that got her attention.

She peered at his ungloved right hand, laying with its palm open, two feet from her.

His fingertips had been burned off.

She glanced at his left hand, but it was covered in a black glove. Something about that bothered her. She wished she could take a closer look.

Tanya racked her memory bank from her recent training.

Criminals scarred their fingertips to avoid identification, but they were usually part of massive organized crime syndicates that were run like corporations. The FBI had sophisticated processes to filter disfigured prints, but they had their limitations. The gangsters knew that.

Was this shooting gang-related?

The officer stepped away from the laptop, shaking his head.

"Are you going to release her now?" said Asha.

The deputy rubbed his chin, then shot a suspicious glance Tanya's way.

"Sheriff can make that decision."

Asha glared at him, then turned to Tanya with an unhappy shake of her head.

Tanya mouthed, "It's OK."

The officer bent down to examine the dead man. Tanya watched as he went through his pockets. Then, suddenly, as if he had just realized something important, he reached over and pried the glove from the man's left hand.

Tanya's eyes widened.

The dead man had the same heart branding on his skin as the homeless kid had.

The officer quickly put the glove back and tucked the hand under the man's shirt, like he didn't want anyone to see it.

He jerked around as if he felt her watching, but Tanya looked away.

Her mind raced.

He recognized that mark. It must mean something important.

The sound of sirens came from the road.

Soon, the café was swarming with deputies in tan uniforms. A middle-aged man with a sheriff's star stepped inside and barked orders at everyone seemingly at once.

Sheriff Reginald was an imposing man with a booming voice and biceps the size of tree trunks. The graying hair and the deep lines on his forehead only made him look more officious.

But even he couldn't control the chaos around him. It was clear to Tanya this bedroom community wasn't prepared to tackle such a horrific crime scene.

One officer stepped on a splotch of blood by the dead woman and only noticed once he started leaving red footprints on the floor.

Cora was talking to anyone who'd listen, gesturing wildly.

"I'm so happy you came, Reginald. You've no idea what happened. I was just getting the last batch of bread out when—"

"Settle down, Cora." The sheriff waved her aside. "I'll get to you shortly."

Cora balked. "I just had this woman ram her car into my shop, kill a man, and shoot herself. And you want me to calm down?"

Through all this pandemonium, Pat and Wyatt remained quietly in their corner.

At first, Tanya thought they were too stunned to move, but the expressions on their faces told her they were watching, listening. Keenly. Their initial fear and panic seemed to have ebbed quickly. This wasn't how normal witnesses reacted.

Before Tanya could say anything to them, a deputy picked her up off the ground, and escorted her out of the café.

That was when Asha pounced on them.

"Look at the camera footage!" she shouted, shoving the laptop in the deputy's face. "Look at this before you take her away."

The sheriff came over, with Cora on his tail, still talking nonstop.

Asha whirled around. "Sheriff, this is a serious miscarriage of justice. You have to see this!"

She blocked his way with the laptop. It took the sheriff three views to conclude he didn't have anything solid to hold Tanya.

"Cut her loose," he barked before giving Tanya a hard look. "I'm going to advise you not to leave town."

"I plan on staying a few days," she replied, her face stoic.

The sheriff frowned. "Where are you from?"

"Seattle."

"What's your business in Paradise Cove?"

"Holiday. We're staying at a friend's house."

He turned to Asha and Katy.

"What about you two?" he boomed. "Where are you from?"

"New York," said Asha.

"What do you do there?"

"I own a baking franchise."

That was Asha's story when she didn't want anyone to know her true vocation as a PI. Since she had established a bakery in Harlem a decade ago, it wasn't a complete lie.

"I work with her," said Katy. "And my husband is a partner with the Schwab, Knowles, and Brighton law firm."

The sheriff's eyebrows shot up. "Is that right?"

He appraised the three women, then stepped back, as if he had misjudged them too quickly. He turned his attention to the deputy who had first arrived at the scene.

"What do we have here, Blake? We know the female, but was there any identification on the male?"

The deputy stood to attention. "Negative, sir. No wallet, no driver's license, nothing. Just the clothes on his back and that gun."

"Anything in the truck?"

"No, sir. We're running the plates right now."

"What's that on his face?"

"It's what they use at the paintball park, down the road. Maybe he came from there."

"At this time of the morning?"

"They're open twenty-four hours, sir. I go there all the time to de-stress."

Tanya rubbed her wrists where the handcuffs had dug in, absorbing the surrounding conversation.

The sheriff glanced at the wreckage and shook his head.

"What in heaven's name happened here?" he said more to himself than anyone else.

Deputy Blake looped his fingers in his belt. "Looks to me like aggressive driving gone real bad, sir. A real extreme case of road rage."

Tanya jerked her head up.

Road rage?

Chapter Eight

"Happens all the time."

Everyone turned to Hudson Wyatt. Tanya could see the man in the suit had clout in this town. He was a man everyone listened to.

"Is that right?" said the sheriff.

"The stats prove it," said Wyatt. "You should read the Seattle papers, Reginald."

"Wish I had the time." The sheriff spat to the side. "Too busy fighting crime, Hudson."

"Road rage hit a record high in Seattle last year. Whether we like it or not, what's happening in the big cities is coming to small towns. People are no longer patient or courteous these days."

"It looked to me like he was chasing her," said Pat in a shaky voice. "She probably cut him off on the road and they ended up here to duke it out."

"Oh, lordy, lordy." Cora rubbed her tired face. "Poor Eveline Hart. What a horrible way to go. What's the world coming to these days?"

The sheriff let out a heavy sigh. "I always say just let the other vehicle pass. There's no need to get upset. You never know who's on the road or what they're carrying."

Tanya looked from Wyatt, to Pat, to Cora, to Deputy Blake, and Sheriff Reginald.

Blake had recognized the strange scar on the dead man's skin, but he hadn't mentioned it to his boss yet. The medical examiner would notice it during the autopsy. It would be on their report, so why pretend not to know what it is?

What was he hiding?

And why was the sheriff so quick to accept such an absurd solution to a horrific crime? There was more going on in Paradise Cove than met the eye.

⸎

Katy pushed her face in between the Jeep's front seats.

"Why didn't you tell them you were FBI?"

Tanya glanced at her friend.

"I'm not on duty."

Asha turned to her from the front passenger seat. "You drew your weapon."

"I didn't fire it."

"Shouldn't you have identified yourself?"

Tanya was silent for a few seconds. "I'd rather ask for forgiveness than permission."

The three of them had given their statements to the deputies and were finally heading to the house where they were going to stay that week.

They had chosen Paradise Cove for their mini-vacation because Katy's foster mother had a home in what had sounded like a quaint seaside location near Seattle. Tanya stopped at a red light, wondering if they had made a big mistake.

"They're all lying," she said. "This town has a secret no one is talking about."

Asha frowned. "Like what?"

"Did you see the man in the truck had the same mark on his hand like Jodie had?"

"Never saw it."

"Me neither," said Katy.

"That's because," said Tanya, "Blake hid it. Only reason I saw it, was because I was on my stomach three feet from the corpse when he pulled off the dead man's glove to take a closer look."

"I'll say this about Deputy Blake," said Katy, poking Tanya in the ribs. "He's one good-looking dude."

"Seriously, Katy?" Tanya rolled her eyes. "Can we focus, please?"

"Didn't Jodie say someone was after him?" said Katy, sounding more thoughtful. "Maybe it was Eveline Hart or that dead man."

"Maybe it was both." Asha nodded. "The kid could have had something they wanted. They could have fought over who was going to get to Jodie first, and that ended in a shootout." She sighed. "It still doesn't explain why Eveline Hart would kill herself."

"Anything makes more sense than this road rage crap," said Tanya, blowing a raspberry. "The sheriff's covering up for something, or he's looking to close a case fast for political expediency."

"You mean, *career* expediency," said Asha, shaking her head.

Tanya had left the crime scene feeling disappointed.

Sheriff Reginald had listened to the witnesses' statements, but seemed to have already made up his mind on the cause of the incident. By the time his deputies had talked to everyone, even Cora had decided it was an extreme case of road rage.

"Eveline shot the man out of sheer anger for following her and crashing into her. Then, she shot herself once she realized what she had done," the sheriff had said with a shrug. "He instigated it, but she took it too far. Human dynamics. It's simple."

"Something's rotten in the state of Denmark," said Asha softly to herself.

"I bet that kid knows what really led to the murder-suicide in the café." Tanya twisted around to Katy. "Did you see where Jodie took off to?"

"He was gone by the time I went looking for him. He even took his buns."

"I don't blame him for running off," said Asha. "He probably thought the cops would lock him up."

"I thought he made up that crazy story about being followed," said Katy, "but I'm not so sure now."

Tanya took the turn toward Sunset Drive. It was a wide, open boulevard with beautifully manicured lawns on either side. Massive mansions were set back on their properties, some partially obscured by fir trees and orchards.

"That burn mark on Jodie's hand," she said, "has to mean something."

"A cult symbol?" said Asha. "There could be one in town."

"It could also be a sign of an organized crime gang."

Katy peered through the window at the colonial manors they were driving by.

"Gangsters in this place? I highly doubt—"

"Look at that!" Asha leaned toward the windshield and pointed. "The big white house with the gabled roof in a cul-de-sac. That must be Eveline Hart's home."

"This is only a block from where we're staying," said Katy.

Tanya slowed to a crawl as they passed the cul-de-sac. Two officers were putting yellow tape around the structure. Other than that, the stately house looked tranquil.

The curtains were drawn and the front door was shut. It was hard to imagine what the inside looked like.

"The burning question," said Tanya, "is who was Eveline Hart, and why did she shoot that man and kill herself?"

Asha tapped her window. "I bet the answers we're looking for are inside that property."

Tanya checked her GPS. They were approaching their home stay in Paradise Cove. She stopped the car in front of their destination and turned the engine off.

"Wow, that's a big house, Katy." Asha peered through her window. "How many people live here?"

"Only my foster mom. She used to take in lost kids until she found it was too much work. There are five bedrooms upstairs and a renovated basement suite. She said to make ourselves at home."

Asha twisted around. "When's she coming back?"

"Two weeks from now. She's in Honduras, building a school for girls. Not her, obviously. She's just there to make sure her money is going where they say it's going."

Katy plucked her handbag from the backseat.

"I don't believe for a moment there's a gang in this town. Not in my mom's suburb."

"Organized crime don't exactly advertise their business," said Tanya. "This is why I didn't want them to know my FBI connection. If anyone is involved in a crime syndicate, and they found out who we all were—"

"Would they have shot us?" said Katy, a wry smile on her lips.

"They'd be more subtle," said Tanya, her face serious. "They'd play along and eventually remove us in a way that won't leave any evidence or alert the authorities."

Asha shuddered. "That sounds sinister."

Tanya turned to her friends.

"This vacation isn't a good idea anymore, girls. Time to say goodbye."

Chapter Nine

K aty gave Tanya an incredulous look.

"You want to end our holiday?"

"Things just got dangerous," said Tanya. "I'm saying this because I love you. I'd never forgive myself if anything happened to you."

"Hold on." Asha put her hand up. "Aren't we overreacting?"

"Did you see what happened in that café?" said Tanya.

"It could have been a personal conflict," said Katy. "A family dispute gone horribly wrong. You're making up a conspiracy where it doesn't exist."

"I have a bad feeling about this place." Tanya tapped a finger on the steering wheel. "I'll pick up Max from the vet and move to a motel, and see what I can dig up."

"Without us?" said Asha.

"I took five days off from work—"

"To hang out with us!" cried Katy.

Asha shook her head. "I'm not going anywhere."

"Asha, David's waiting for you to come home," said Tanya. "Katy, I'm sure Chantal misses you and wants you to tuck her in at night. Catch a flight back to New York tonight. You have families. You're civilians."

"For goodness' sake," scoffed Katy. "This isn't a war zone."

"If we hadn't been with you today," said Asha, "you'd be spending the night in jail until they watched the security footage. That could have taken days. Weeks."

"I can handle that," said Tanya. "This is my job."

"This isn't an FBI case. You just want it to be."

Katy poked Tanya. "You're worried you're going to have to babysit us."

"Never said that."

"You're thinking it."

"We fought traffickers before we were of legal age to drink," said Asha, her voice rising. "We've been in worse situations. Don't you have faith in us?"

Katy put a hand on Tanya's shoulder.

"You're so wound up, you've become paranoid. You need to learn to relax, hun." She paused. "I say this with a lot of love. I think it's high time you start dating again."

Tanya turned to her, eyes narrowed. "*What?*"

"Properly dating, not just hooking up like you do," said Asha. "Then, maybe start a family—"

Tanya rolled her eyes. "You're my family. An annoying one at that."

"You have no life," said Katy. "Ask that cute cop out for a drink. I saw how he looked at you when he was putting on the handcuffs."

Tanya threw her hands in the air. "What's wrong with you two?"

"We're only saying this for your good," huffed Katy.

"I look like Furiosa from *Mad Max* on a good day."

"Charlize Theron on a bad day, you mean," said Asha, poking her in the ribs. "That's not such a bad thing."

Tanya shook her head. "I'm too intense, too serious, too tall, too everything. No one wants a serious relationship with someone like me. I'm nothing like you two."

"Oh, for heaven's sake, play me a sad violin," said Katy. "Maybe you haven't noticed I'm *fat*."

"Curvaceously gorgeous."

"And I'm short," said Asha.

"Petite and pretty." Tanya turned to her friends and glared. "Why are we even having this juvenile conversation? Can we get back on the topic, please?"

Asha grumbled and Katy looked away.

"You two head home tonight," said Tanya, her voice firm.

"Sure," said Katy, her voice dripping in sarcasm. "Book me a flight out."

"I'm a detective," said Asha. "If you think I'm going to ignore a horrific murder-suicide which everyone believes is road—"

"Hey!" Katy cut her off and pointed as a white Mercedes sedan passed them. "Don't we know her?"

The car drove up the driveway of the house next to theirs.

"That's Pat," said Asha, putting her window down. "The woman with the cane at the café."

"Is she our neighbor?" Katy opened the door. "Let's go say hello."

"Time to start our investigation," said Asha, following her out.

Tanya stayed in the Jeep, shaking her head, watching them stroll over to Pat's driveway.

She didn't trust that woman. She didn't trust anyone in this town. And she really wished she didn't have to watch over her friends.

They weren't just her best friends since childhood, they were her only family left. If anything happened to them, she would never forgive herself.

Pat got out of her car and stood shakily, holding on to her cane. With her pinched mouth and austere expression, she looked like she loathed the entire planet.

She opened the rear car door and pushed her head inside, as if to reach for something. Asha and Katy approached her car, friendly smiles on their faces.

"Hi there," called out Asha.

Pat whirled around, a scowl on her face.

"Hi Pat, we're staying at—"

Katy didn't get to finish. The woman's face turned an alarming tinge of purple.

"Get out of my driveway!"

Asha and Katy stepped away from her, shocked looks on their faces. Pat swatted the air with her walking stick, like she was shooing away unwanted insects.

Tanya stepped out of her vehicle.

"Didn't mean to bother you—" Katy started.

"It's you out-of-towners who brought this trouble on us. Go away."

Tanya walked up to her friends, who were now backing off.

Pat pointed her cane at their home stay next door. "Is that Airbnb even legal? I'm complaining to the city."

Katy's face flushed. "That's my foster mother's home. We're housesitting for her. We're not strangers."

"You are all strangers to me." Pat slammed her car door shut and limped up the driveway toward her front door. "Vagrants! Get out of my town. You're not welcome here."

Asha and Katy turned away, red faced.

Tanya shook her head.

"So much for trying to be neighborly."

They were walking back to the Jeep when the green Jaguar zoomed past them. It pulled into a massive brick house set back on an enormous property across the street. A sign posted on the lawn swung from the gust of wind.

Tanya squinted and read the sign out aloud.

"Re-elect Councilor Wyatt."

"So the man's on the city council." Asha hauled her bag out of the back of the Jeep. "That's why the sheriff was ready to believe him before us, out-of-towners, as Pat so lovingly calls us."

"Just look at that mansion," said Katy. "He's got the ocean on the other side. Do you think we can convince him to invite us over?"

"I don't know if I'd want to go," said Asha. "But I wouldn't mind a convertible like that myself."

Tanya's eyes narrowed. "I'd like to know how he came to all that wealth."

"Not everyone who's rich is a gang member, Tanya," said Katy. "You two need to rein in your judging."

Tanya reached into her cargo pants pocket, plucked her phone out, and typed Hudson Wyatt's name into the search bar of the browser. She let out a low whistle.

"He's the younger son of the richest family in the county."

Katy peeked over her arm. "What do they do?"

"Lumber. They ship to China, Japan, and Germany. They've made a fortune over the years."

"They're the ones killing the West Coast rain forest?" Asha made a face. "I like him even less now."

Tanya scrolled down. "Hudson Wyatt's the founding family's only son. He has a Harvard law degree but doesn't seem to have a practice." She stopped. "His older sister runs the lumber company now."

"Shouldn't he be somewhere warm?" said Katy. "On a beach surrounded by pretty girls in bikinis and a margarita in his hand? It's not like he needs to work."

"Some people are driven by more than the need to sit on a beach and do nothing all day," said Asha.

"Well, that's what I'd do if I had that kind of money," said Katy. "Sans the girls in bikinis, of course." She smiled. "Maybe a few bare-chested hot dudes in tiny shorts."

Asha gave her a friendly punch. "I won't tell Peace you said that."

Tanya kept scrolling through news articles about the Wyatt family. "It's strange why a single young man would want to live by himself in a mansion with only a Great Dane to keep him company."

"How do you know he's single?" said Katy.

"Cora at the café told me. He's supposedly the most eligible bachelor in the area."

Asha and Katy rolled their eyes.

Tanya stopped scrolling.

"Whoa."

"What?" said Asha.

"Money trouble," said Tanya, pulling up a recent article. "The company filed for bankruptcy this year."

"That would explain why he isn't on a beach, sipping a cocktail," said Asha in a dry voice.

The sound of footsteps came from across the street.

"Speaking of the devil," said Tanya.

"Oooh," whispered Katy, whirling around, flustered. "He's coming over!"

Asha spun toward the Jeep and pretended to fiddle with their luggage.

Chapter Ten

"Hello ladies. We meet again."

Tanya, Asha, and Katy turned around, innocent expressions on their faces. Wyatt strolled up to them, a bright smile on his face and his dog in tow.

His eyes flitted toward Asha, and drifted from her face, to her chest, to her thighs. Tanya could see her discomfort and shook her head.

Why do some men do this? Don't they realize it makes our skin crawl?

Katy gave him a friendly wave. "Hi again. I guess we'll be neighbors."

"Are you ladies visiting?"

"A short vacation."

He offered his hand to Katy.

"I couldn't ask for better neighbors than three pretty young ladies like you."

Instead of shaking Katy's hand, Wyatt bowed over it and kissed it.

He even acts like an old-fashioned dude from the seventeenth century.

Asha bent to pet the dog, more to fend off a smarmy kiss from the man than anything else. "What a gorgeous pup."

Wyatt looked down at his dog, and his face softened.

"Isn't he?" He gave an embarrassed chuckle. "You must think I'm a bit off driving around town with a Great Dane in my open car."

Yes, I do.

"We love pups," said Katy. "Our dog's at the vet, but he'll be coming home soon. He really belongs to Tanya, but we have all claimed him as family."

Wyatt turned to Tanya, curiosity in his eyes. "What's his breed?"

Tanya couldn't get away from this man fast enough, but he was waiting for an answer.

"German Shepherd."

"Mixed with a bit of husky," said Asha.

Wyatt leaned toward them, his face turning serious, like he was about to divulge a secret.

"Listen, I saw how Pat spoke to you. Don't take it to heart. She's not been feeling well lately."

"What's wrong with her?" said Katy.

"She's had more than her fair share of bad luck."

"Does she live alone?" said Tanya.

Wyatt nodded. "Ever since her daughter ran away and her husband passed about three years ago."

He looked away as if he was embarrassed to be sharing this information, but Tanya could see he was dying to talk.

Contrary to popular belief, she knew men enjoyed gossiping just as much as women did. Maybe even more. Wyatt didn't disappoint. He leaned in again and lowered his voice.

"Her husband was a nuclear physicist. Worked for a large science corporation and wrote a bestseller on the Manhattan Project. It was quite a shock to the scientific community when he died. He had a severe heart attack before he even hit forty."

"How sad," said Katy.

"It's why I live a stress-free life." Wyatt bent down to stroke his dog's head. "I don't plan to drop dead like these overworked corporate execs."

"What does Pat do?" said Tanya.

"She was an English professor at the South Seattle University. Published several books herself. I believe she went on an extended sabbatical after her husband died, then took early retirement. She took it hard."

Katy put her hands on her hips.

"That's decided then. I'm going to visit her with muffins tomorrow morning. Maybe that will soften her up."

A strange smile cut across Wyatt's face.

"You do that. She'll appreciate the gesture." He paused. "If you ladies need anything, just knock on my door. I'm at your service. Enjoy your stay in Paradise Cove."

With a small bow, he turned around and strolled back to his house.

They watched him walk away, his long-legged canine companion padding behind him.

"Something's odd about him," whispered Asha. "Quirky."

"Slimy," said Tanya. "Slimy is the word you're looking for."

"Stop staring, you two," said Katy, nudging them. "He's just being neighborly. Let's go inside and open a bottle of wine. Heaven knows I need one."

Without waiting for her friends, Katy rolled her suitcase up the driveway, toward the front door of her foster mother's house.

Asha pulled the handle from her suitcase and followed her. Tanya clicked her key fob to lock the Jeep and joined Asha. They were halfway up the driveway when a chilling scream came from Pat's house.

They dropped their bags and were about to run over when a frightened shout came from inside their own home.

"Help! Someone help!"

"Katy!" cried Asha, whirling around.

Tanya burst through the front door first.

"What happened? You all right?"

Katy was standing in the kitchen, staring out the back window, a hand over her mouth.

Tanya stepped up to her. "What is it?"

"Oh, my gosh," said Asha as she dashed over. "It's Jodie, the kid."

The homeless boy they had met at the café was lying prone in Pat's backyard, clutching the sugar buns to his chest. He was still, but even from where they were, they could see the foam frothing from his bluish mouth.

Tanya spun on her heels and ran out the back door, shouting.

"Call nine-one-one!"

She jumped the fence to Pat's backyard, barely registering the woman's pale face staring from the porch.

Ask for forgiveness rather than permission.

She raced over to the boy.

"Hey, Jodie!" she called out as she reached for his shoulder. "Jodie, are you okay?"

She touched his wrists, then his neck, but felt no pulse. His skin was cold and clammy. Tanya stared at the body, certain the boy had taken his last breath before Katy had even spotted him.

Asha and Katy came over.

"Ambulance is on its way," said Asha.

Tanya turned to her companions with a grim look. "It's too late."

They stood around the boy in silent vigil, sorrow overtaking them, even though they had barely known the kid.

"Where's his hoodie?" said Asha, glancing around.

Tanya shrugged. "Could have lost it."

"What's that in his hand?"

Katy was pointing at the kid's hand with the scar. Tanya bent down and gently pried his fingers open. Held inside was a yellow plastic vial.

"Pills?" said Katy, bending over to look. "He didn't have it on him at the café."

"Could have been in his pocket," said Asha.

Tanya scrutinized the small white tablets in the container, making sure to not touch it. "I would bet my entire salary this is Fentanyl. Two milligrams of this and it's lethal."

"Someone could have given it to him after he left the café," said Asha.

"What I want to know is what was he doing in Pat's backyard," said Tanya.

"What happened?"

They whirled around to see Pat standing a few feet from them, swaying on her feet, her cane forgotten.

"What's going on?" she croaked. "What happened to him?"

Asha turned toward her. "The boy's dead."

Pat clutched her chest.

Tanya leaped toward her, but was too late. Pat crashed to the ground with a hard thud.

Chapter Eleven

"Wake up!"

Tanya shook Katy by the shoulder.

"Hey, Katy, wake up."

Katy turned away and snuggled deeper into her pillow. "Lemme sleep."

Tanya had slept little that evening.

She usually never did.

Her PTSD flared up every nightfall. The faces of the monsters she killed in her youth flashed across her mind like a silent horror flick every night.

Every life she had taken had been in defense of an abused child, a trafficked victim, or a broken woman used as a punching bag. The wounded, the forgotten, the innocents. But that never seemed to wash off the blood she had on her hands.

That evening, it was Jodie's murder that weighed most heavily on her mind. It hadn't been an accidental drug overdose. Someone had wanted that kid gone.

Tanya felt responsible for what happened to Jodie. She had tossed and turned, the kid's frightened face lodged in her head, until she sat up and made a promise to herself.

I'm going to find out who killed him.

She had little faith in the local law enforcement crew.

Deputy Blake had driven over to Pat's house with a partner. While the paramedics had attended to Pat, who had fainted, the deputies had taped off the backyard and told Tanya, Asha, and Katy to step away and stay away.

All they could do was watch from the other side of the fence as the two officers bumbled their way around the crime scene.

They had homed in on the yellow vial.

"Another opioid death," Deputy Blake had said, shaking his head. "Second this month. There's only so much we can do."

His partner had seemed to agree.

Tanya had wanted to demand they check the vial for fingerprints, the buns for poison, and the lawn for footprints. They had to interview Pat, who had probably witnessed what had happened, or might have known something.

Neither officer had seemed keen to take advice from a potential suspect who had been in handcuffs only a few hours ago.

But it was one in the morning now, and Tanya had a more urgent problem at hand. Asha had disappeared, and she didn't know how or where she was.

She shook Katy by the arm again.

"Get up!"

Katy turned around and slowly opened her eyes. "What time is it?"

Tanya got up from the bed with a frustrated hiss. "Where's Asha?"

Katy sat up and blinked.

"What do you mean? She's not in her room?"

"I thought I heard something a few minutes ago. I checked the entire house. Everything's locked tight, but when I looked into her room, she wasn't there."

"Maybe she's in the bathroom?"

"Don't you think I checked?" Tanya shot her an irate look. "Did you two hatch something without telling me?"

"Of course not. We'd never do that."

"Like that never happened before."

"I swear, we aren't doing anything behind your back." Katy pulled off the covers. "We need to call the pol—"

Tanya's phone buzzed, making Katy jump. Tanya checked her cell and cursed.

"What?" Katy scrambled out of the bed. "Is she okay?"

"You won't believe what that girl's up to."

"What?"

"Investigating." Tanya made air quotes with her hand. "She left fifteen minutes ago."

Katy blinked rapidly, her groggy brain slowly waking up.

"She's at Eveline's home, isn't she? She was talking about that house all afternoon."

Tanya's frown deepened.

"Why didn't she tell me?" Katy fumbled for her slippers. "I would have gone with her—hey, where are you off to?"

But Tanya had already left the room.

Katy whirled around and picked up the pair of jeans she had tossed on the back of a chair.

"Wait for me!"

Tanya was by the front door, checking her weapon, when Katy scrambled down the stairs.

"Where are you heading?"

"Going to grab that woman, shake her hard, and bring her home safely," said Tanya, pulling her jacket on. "You stay right here."

"Are you nuts? I'm not staying here by myself while you and Asha go off to solve the case."

Tanya looked at Katy's obstinate face and sighed. Their found family came from different backgrounds, but they all shared one common trait. They were stubborn as heck. Tanya knew it was useless to argue when either Katy or Asha had made up their minds.

"Soft shoes and gloves."

She opened the front door and stepped outside. Katy put on her canvas shoes, stuffed her gloves in her pocket, and scurried after her.

An eerie quietness had settled on Sunset Drive.

"What was she thinking?" muttered Tanya as she stomped down the driveway, her Glock in hand.

"Brrr," said Katy, hugging herself. She picked up her pace to keep up with her friend's long strides.

It took them two minutes to walk to the cul-de-sac where Eveline Hart's home was.

"Stay back," said Tanya, pushing Katy behind an oak tree from across the house.

The waning moonlight was enough to make out the neighborhood. All the nearby residences had plunged into darkness, their inhabitants presumably asleep. The enormous homes on the street now looked like strange monsters looming over them.

"Stick to the hedges on the east," said Tanya, stepping out from behind the tree. "It'll give us cover."

"What about the cops?" whispered Katy.

"I expected them to have security at night too, but it seems like they're relying on the yellow tape to keep trespassers at bay."

"I guess no one from this neighborhood would be sneaking around like us," said Katy.

"Speak for yourself," said Tanya. "I'm doing this under duress."

She crossed the street and darted over to the cedar hedge that ran the length of the property. Keeping to the shadows, she threaded to the back of Eveline Hart's house, with Katy at her heels.

The yellow tape was draped across the kitchen door, but Tanya could see someone had moved it. All the curtains in the back had been pulled open as if to let the moonlight in.

Is Asha in there?

Cursing her friend, Tanya tiptoed to the kitchen window and peered inside.

"See anything?" whispered Katy.

Tanya stepped toward the back door and turned the doorknob. It was unlocked.

"Coming?"

Katy glanced around her, seeing dark shadows dancing in the corners of the backyard. She hugged herself and nodded.

Tanya stepped inside. Katy followed her in and closed the door behind her.

They didn't need much light to see the house had been turned upside down.

Cupboards and drawers had been flung open. Expensive china, silver cutlery, spice containers, and tins of coffee and sugar had been thrown on the floor.

Katy inched closer to Tanya, like she was worried someone would snatch her in the dark.

"Someone was searching for something," whispered Tanya.

"What a mess," said Katy, as her eyes adjusted to the dim light and the mayhem became even more surreal. "It's like a tornado went through here."

Tanya could feel a presence in the house. She just hoped it would be their friend.

"Eveline Hart had some nice things," Katy was saying. "That gold vase is the only thing left intact. Must have cost a fortune—"

The thud of a drawer closing came from somewhere on the first floor. Tanya and Katy exchanged a glance.

Is that Asha?

Could it be someone else?

Tanya put her finger to her lips. She tiptoed around the clutter and crept down the hallway that led to the rest of the house.

A lone figure was rummaging through a cabinet drawer in a corner of the living room. They were so focused on their task, they hadn't noticed Tanya and Katy creep up from behind.

Tanya wanted to call out, but it was hard to say who it was.

She treaded around the wall and stepped inside the living room to get a better look.

The figure whipped around.

In the pale moonlight, Tanya saw the flash of a steel knife charge toward her stomach.

Chapter Twelve

Tanya leaped to the side.

"Asha! It's us!"

Tanya turned on her flashlight. Asha was shielding her eyes, blinking rapidly.

"Oh, my gosh," cried Katy, a hand on her chest. "Thank goodness, you're okay."

Tanya lowered her weapon and glared at her friend. Asha was clutching what looked like a can of bear spray in a gloved hand. Her knife had slid halfway across the living room now.

Asha gave Tanya a crossed look.

"Why did you sneak up on me like that?"

"I wasn't sure if it was you or someone else," said Tanya.

"You aren't supposed to be here."

"Neither are you."

"I'm looking for the truth, unlike the sheriff and his clowns."

Tanya threw her arms in the air. "You're the one with the steady head. You always kept me in line. What happened to you?"

Asha shot her an obstinate look. "I became a private investigator, and you became a government agent."

Tanya shook her head. "I thought we agreed. No more vigilante jobs."

"I work for myself now. No one tells me what to do."

"Unlike you, I have rules to follow."

"That's why I told you not to come looking for me."

"I came here to save your skin! What do you think your kitchen knife and pepper spray would have done if someone snuck up on you with a gun, like I did?"

"Now that you mention it, I wish I brought my Glock—"

"Smuggle it across state lines?"

Katy held a hand up. "All right, you two. Stop it." She turned to Asha. "Don't ever take off on me in the middle of the night like this. You almost gave me a heart attack. Tell me first, next time."

Tanya's eyebrows shot up. *Next time?*

"The good thing," said Katy, "is no one's hurt."

Asha winced. "Other than the bump on my head."

"How did you get in here?" said Tanya. "Didn't the deputies lock up?"

"I jimmied the lock," said Asha.

"Break and enter, you mean?"

"I learned from you." Asha drew out a tension wrench from her pants pocket and turned to Katy. "Your foster mom's house is well stocked."

Tanya closed her eyes and summoned all the patience she had. She and David had taught their family members the basic tactics they had learned while working for the Mossad and CIA. But there were days when she regretted it.

This was one of them.

"Pack up your knife and wrench, Nancy Drew," said Tanya. "We're going home pronto. I should have you arrested."

Asha turned to her. "Did you see Eveline Hart's face when she shot herself? I can't get that image out of my head. I can't sleep."

She looked away, her face troubled.

"Something terrible happened to her. I need to know what it was. We should figure it out and bring some justice to the memory of that poor woman. Those cops won't do anything."

No one spoke for a few seconds. They had all felt the same, but no one else had articulated it. But now, it was out in the open.

"Someone ransacked this place looking for something important," said Asha. "They didn't find it and neither did the police. They all missed it."

"How do you know that?" said Katy.

A sly expression came over Asha's face. "Because I found it."

Tanya and Katy stared at her.

"You won't believe what Eveline Hart was hiding in the pantry."

"What did you find?" said Tanya, despite herself.

"Easier to show than explain." Asha gestured to her friends. "Follow me."

"Wait." Tanya stepped out in front of her. "Let me secure the house first."

"I've been here almost half an hour, and I haven't seen anyone."

"Doesn't mean someone isn't hiding on the premises."

Tanya gestured toward the back door. "Wait there till I give the all-clear. If you see or hear anything from the outside, call me. If you hear a gunshot from inside, run."

She stepped away from her friends, before they could object.

With every step she took, Tanya could feel her blood pressure rise. *This is a crime scene,* her brain kept screaming. *We shouldn't be here.*

We're not kids anymore, fighting to stay alive. We're adults in a free country. And I'm a federal agent now, for heaven's sake.

Tanya could no longer justify rogue investigations, but despite her reticence, her curiosity about what Asha had discovered was slowly overcoming her.

Just one quick look shouldn't hurt.

It took her ten minutes to sweep the property, but apart from them, the house was empty.

As soon as Tanya gave the all-clear, Asha led them through the kitchen and into the pantry. Once inside, she turned on her phone's flashlight.

"Turn that off," said Tanya.

"No one can see in here." Asha shone her light on the back wall of the pantry and tapped on a wooden panel. "See this? This is a false door."

Katy's eyebrows shot up. "How on earth did you figure that out?"

Asha swung her flashlight to the floor.

"See these huge rice sacks? They expired two years ago. No one was planning on cooking them."

Tanya knitted her brows.

"Look at these stacks of potato and onion bags on top of the rice," said Asha. "Whoever was searching the house didn't move them. They just slashed a few to check inside, but left them in place."

She turned to her friends.

"There had to be a good reason these were stacked along the back wall like this."

"This is a pantry," said Tanya. "It's where people normally keep dry goods."

"But everybody knows you're not supposed to store potatoes with onions."

"I didn't know that."

"You're not everybody," said Katy to Tanya. "Potatoes get bad faster when they're next to onions."

"They're props," said Asha, handing her knife and phone to Katy. "No one was going to eat this stuff."

She turned back to the wall and hauled a dozen sacks aside before pushing on the wooden panel.

It swung open.

"A secret door," gasped Katy.

Asha stepped in through the narrow entrance. Katy and Tanya followed, ducking under the low doorway.

It was midnight black inside. Tanya pulled her phone out, turned on the flashlight, and rotated it slowly around the windowless, closet-sized room.

On the wall in front of them was a large cork board.

On it, were photocopies of newspaper clippings, maps, photographs, and sheets of paper with illegible handwriting, connected by red string crisscrossing each other haphazardly.

"My gosh," whispered Katy. "What is this?"

"A murder board," said Tanya.

Chapter Thirteen

K aty pointed at the board.

"Is that *Jodie*?"

"A recent photo," said Asha. "With his hoodie and wig."

Tanya scrutinized the black and white photocopy. It was out of focus and looked like someone had snapped it from a street corner without his knowledge.

She moved her flashlight to the middle of the board.

The blurry faces of two middle-aged men took a prominent spot in the center. They looked like typical suburban dads you might find at a baseball game, but their photocopied headshots had been circled with a thick red marker and a dot in the middle.

Bull's eye.

Tanya moved her light down.

A row of six printed headshots had been pinned to the bottom of the corkboard. They were boys, in their early teens, staring at the camera, confusion etched on their faces.

Tanya focused her light on the photo at the end. It was a pixelated print image of a digital photo, and as fuzzy as the others.

It was hard to make out the features, but something about it nagged at her.

"Wait, this is a girl. I'm sure of it."

Katy put a finger on the second picture. "Is it just me or does this one look familiar?"

They stared at the face. The boy was thirteen or fourteen, at most.

"Looks like Jodie," said Asha, "but younger. Could it be his brother?"

"Or maybe Jodie when he was a kid?" said Katy, frowning.

"I knew there was a connection between Jodie's death and Eveline's murder-suicide in the café," said Asha. "This proves it."

"But how are they connected?" said Katy. "And who was that man in the truck?"

"I haven't figured everything out yet," said Asha.

Tanya turned to her friends. "We have to report this to the sheriff ASAP."

"He sounds corrupt or incompetent," said Asha.

"Even if that's true, we can't hide evidence from the county sheriff. That's a felony that will get us all in trouble."

Asha's eyes flashed in the dark. "I don't care if I get arrested, I won't stop until I figure out what happened to Eveline Hart. There had to be a reason she killed herself like that."

"She committed homicide," said Tanya in a low voice.

"I was looking through the café window when she shot him. She was so angry, she was shaking. I want answers for her sake."

"It was like watching a horror movie," said Katy, her voice somber, "except it was real. I still don't think I've come to terms with what happened."

"The local crew won't do anything. They'll shove it under the rug." Asha stepped back, raised her phone, and snapped photos of the board.

"If Sheriff Reginald is a good cop," she said, "he'll thank us for finding this."

"I doubt Blake and his crew even thought of looking for a secret compartment behind expired food sacks," said Katy.

"My worry is," said Tanya with a heavy sigh, "he could charge us with tampering with evidence, breaking and entering, trespassing on private property, you name it."

Katy fingered a stack of crinkled papers that had been pinned together on the board.

"Newspaper clippings," she murmured, flipping through the yellowed paper. "From the Seattle area." She pulled the stack out.

"You can't remove those," said Tanya.

"I'm just going to lay them out in the kitchen counter and snap a few photos," said Katy, "for our investigation."

"We have no official investigation."

"You don't," said Katy, stepping out of the pantry. "We do."

Tanya turned back to the board and shook her head. She was glad they were all wearing gloves. The last thing she wanted was to have important clues get smudged by their fingers or have their fingerprints on the evidence.

Asha stepped up to the board. "Katy forgot a clipping."

She pried off the faded piece of paper that had been stuck to the board. Tanya looked over her shoulder. Written in scraggly letters was a list of names with dates next to them.

"Liam, Noel, Matt, Peter, Jodie."

"Jodie?" Asha's eyebrows shot up. "That young boy's photo is him, then. But what do these dates mean? The day they were killed?"

"Jodie died yesterday but the date next to him is three years ago."

"So, it's when they were taken? Kidnapped?"

Tanya's brain whirred, but she had no definite answers to any of the questions her friends were asking.

"Who are these kids?" Asha whispered to herself.

"The big question is why are they on a murder board?" said Tanya. "Whatever happened to them, Eveline was tracking them."

A flash of aquamarine on the floor caught her eye. She bent down to pick it up, shook off the dust, and held it up.

"A beaded necklace?" said Asha.

Tanya turned to the photos of the children. The kid who looked like a girl was wearing a similar choker.

"A memento?" said Asha.

"Serial offenders like to track their crimes and save keepsakes from their victims," said Tanya in a thoughtful voice.

Asha gasped. "Was Eveline Hart a serial killer?"

Tanya frowned. Somehow, that didn't sound logical.

But Asha was getting animated.

"The man in the truck found out about her secret activities. That's why he came after her. He could have been a family member of one of her victims. An older brother to one of these kids, maybe."

"But why kill herself?" said Tanya.

"Remorse, regret, shock over what she'd done. Maybe the sheriff was right after all, except the reasoning is different."

Tanya shook her head.

"It's rare for a female unsub to kill children that don't belong to her. When kids are murdered, it's usually after years of abuse and neglect by a parent or a family member."

Tanya's frown deepened.

"This doesn't add up. A murder board is made by someone who doesn't know what's going on. It's a tool to connect the dots and solve a puzzle. If Eveline was kidnapping or killing children, why would she create—"

A crash came from the kitchen, startling them.

Katy!

Chapter Fourteen

Tanya leaped through the narrow opening and into the pantry.

She rushed into the kitchen to see Katy staring in horror at a pile of broken glass on the floor.

Katy snapped her head up. "I saw a face!"

Tanya whirled around, her gun at the ready.

"Where?"

"In the back window. I think it was a man. He disappeared into the woods."

"Someone was watching us?" said Asha.

Tanya stepped over to the back window and scoured the yard.

While Paradise Cove was nestled against the shore, only the houses on the south side had views of the water. That included Hudson Wyatt's mansion. Eveline Hart's house was set against the woods on the other side, like their own home stay.

Tanya's eyes darted back and forth, trying to penetrate the tree line at the end of the yard. Even with the moonlight streaming onto the trees, it was difficult to see if anyone was hiding in there.

She turned to her friends. "We need to leave now."

"What do I do about this?" Katy pointed at the shattered glass in dismay. "I elbowed the vase by accident when I saw the spy."

"The golden vase?" gasped Asha. "That must have cost thousands."

Katy nodded forlornly.

"If the crew documented the evidence and took photos, they'd notice the missing vase right away," said Tanya. "We have to fess up before they find this."

Katy put her hand on her face.

"Lies have a way of coming back to haunt you," said Tanya, a warning in her voice. "An omission is a type of—"

"Hey!" Asha cut her off. "What's *this*?"

She stepped over to the counter where the golden vase had stood only moments ago.

Tanya squinted. "That's an air vent."

"An air vent on the kitchen counter?" said Asha. "They're normally installed by the floorboards."

"It sucks out the cooking smells," said Katy.

Asha pointed at the powerful stainless steel fan hanging from the ceiling above the stove. "That's what that's for. This is something else."

She pushed the corners of the plastic vent and stepped back as the cover came off and fell into her open hands.

"A hidden safe," gasped Katy.

"They sell these for a hundred and fifty bucks online. I installed one at a client's home a few months ago for her high-end jewelry."

Asha placed the vent cover down and reached inside. "Cards. A stack of cards." She extricated them and placed them on the counter. "No, these are photographs."

Tanya and Katy peered over her shoulder.

"Who prints photos, anymore?" said Katy. "Don't people save them on a computer or a phone these days?"

Asha picked up the first photo of two baby boys with blue ribbons around their heads. They looked happy and angelic as they cuddled together on a fuzzy white throw.

"Ooh, baby pics," said Katy, clasping her hands. "They're adorable."

"These are old." Asha flipped through the stack, glancing at them before placing them on the counter in a row.

"The question is who are they?" said Tanya, examining the latest one Asha pulled out. "And why stuff them in a secret drawer in the kitchen?"

Asha looked up as if a thought had struck her.

"I scoped out all the rooms when I first came in and didn't spot one photo, framed or otherwise. I thought it was odd at first, then I was sure the person or people who ransacked the house stole them, but—"

"They were hidden in the kitchen all along." Katy completed her sentence.

They stared at the baby photos on the counter. Asha looked at the stack in her hands and pulled the next one out.

"Hey, that looks like Eveline Hart in the middle," said Katy, pointing.

Tanya plucked it from Asha's hands and flipped it over. She squinted at the words written on the back. It was hard to read with the limited moonlight that streamed through the back windows, but she didn't dare turn on her phone.

She read the words out loud. "To my lovely wife, Eveline, and my dear sons, Sam, and Eric."

"Must be Eveline Hart's husband and two sons," said Katy. "The boys must be grown now. These look like they were taken ages ago."

Tanya scrolled to the photographs she had snapped inside the pantry.

"I don't think these two boys are on the board."

Asha flipped through the stack of photos, spreading them on the counter.

"Seems like it's all the same people. This one's on a sailboat. Hiking in a park. At a tropical beach. At Christmas dinner. Looks like a happy fam—"

Asha stopped and brought the last photo closer to her eyes. It was a more recent one and the two boys looked to be in their late teens now.

She put the photo down. "Are my eyes playing games or do you recognize one of the young men?"

"It's too dark to see," said Katy, tapping her phone.

"No lights, please," said Tanya.

"Don't worry." Katy placed her phone over the photo. "We take a picture, zoom in on it, and voila...."

Asha waited for her friends to see the resemblance.

Katy gave Asha a shocked look. "Eveline shot her own *son*?"

"If these two are her sons, that is," said Asha.

Tanya recalled Deputy Blake hiding the dead man's hand. "Why do I feel the townsfolk knew who he was but didn't admit to it?"

"An even more disturbing question," said Asha, "is why would a mother murder her own son?"

Tanya scooped the photos and placed them inside the hidden drawer on the wall, before replacing the vent cover.

"We'll figure out what to do about all this tomorrow."

Katy nodded. "This place is getting creepier by the minute."

73

"I get the feeling that if we poke around some more we'll find dead bodies behind these walls," said Asha.

They put everything back in place, locked the back door, and got back on the street.

They threaded in single file toward their home with Tanya in the rear. They stuck to the shadows, hoping none of the neighbors would see them and call the police.

"What's she doing up at this time?" said Tanya when they reached their driveway.

Asha and Katy turned to look. A yellow light shone through their immediate neighbor's back window. Through the sheer curtains, they could see a dark silhouette of a woman leaning on a cane.

"Pat," said Katy. "She's recovered fast, hasn't she?"

"Recovered enough to snoop at us out-of-towners," said Asha.

"Keep it down," whispered Tanya from behind. "I don't like us being out in the open like this. Anyone could target us."

It was a relief to get in the house and lock the door behind them. Asha went to the kitchen to get a glass of water while Tanya started a security check of the house.

Katy flopped down on the living room couch. "I'm going to crash right here—"

"Hey, come here!"

Tanya was in the basement when she heard Asha call out. She tore up the steps, her heart beating a tick faster.

"Everyone okay?"

"Who would do such a thing?" came Katy's frightened voice from the kitchen.

Tanya dashed into the kitchen to see her friends staring at the back window.

"Another body on Pat's lawn?" she asked.

Asha and Katy parted. The kitchen window looked grimy at first glance, dirtier than Tanya had seen it before.

"Somebody doesn't want us in Paradise Cove," said Asha, tapping the glass.

Tanya stared at the scribbles made by a red marker. The words were crooked and had been written by someone standing on the outside, so she had to read them backward.

Go home. Or you'll end up like the boy.

"They mean Jodie, don't they?" said Katy.

Tanya nodded gravely. "That confirms his death was suspicious."

Asha snapped a photo of the message. "I bet Pat wrote this while we were away."

Katy gave a disgusted tsk. "And here I was going to make her muffins tomorrow."

"I don't think it's her," said Tanya.

She peered through the window. Pat's house had turned dark, but that didn't mean she wasn't watching from a corner of a window somewhere.

"Why not?" said Katy. "She's the one who told us to go home, just like this note."

"She couldn't have come here," said Tanya, "unless that cane is a prop."

Day Two

Chapter Fifteen

Tanya scrambled to pick up her phone on the bed stand.

She stared at the word scrolling across the screen. *Restricted.*

She knew who that was.

It was six on a Saturday morning and she was on vacation. *What does work want with me?* She accepted the call.

"Agent Stone?"

"Stone here."

Tanya threw her legs over the covers and stood up. It was still heart-stopping to be called *Agent.*

"I have a case I'd like you to take on." It was Paul Desmond, Special Agent in Charge, her immediate supervisor at the Seattle field office.

"I can come in right away." Tanya picked up her soiled T-shirt from the floor and glanced at her open bag, hoping she had brought one of her button-down shirts.

"I've been called to a meeting with the director on Monday," said Desmond. "I'd like to brief you soon after. Can you be in my office at fourteen hundred hours, Tuesday?"

"Roger that," said Tanya.

That gives me forty-eight hours to find out what happened to Jodie and those kids.

"I'll be there, sir."

"I'm sorry to cut your holiday short, Stone," said Desmond. "But I knew I could count on you."

Tanya noticed a hint of relief in his voice. She wondered if senior agents balked at leaving vacations early, but she didn't have a choice.

"May I ask what this is about? Anything I can do to prepare?"

She winced as she heard her own eager beaver voice. This wasn't her usual character, but she was a rookie at the bureau and still on probation, which meant they could let her go at a moment's notice.

She needed this job. Desperately.

"Director Cross hasn't shared details with me, yet," said Desmond. "What I know is she wants someone with multi-faceted skills, preferably a former vet, and capable of handling a solo mission. This will require travel."

Tanya's eyebrows shot up.

They never send new agents on solo missions.

The FBI recruitment office had waived the age requirement for her as a veteran. But she had felt like the ugly duckling in a sea of fresh-faced, twenty-something-year-old swans who were starting out in their careers and their lives.

"Will I be needing Max?" asked Tanya.

"How's he doing?"

"Routine neutering operation. He's already had a day to recover at the vet. I'll be picking him up today. He should be back to normal in a couple of days. "

"The K9 unit chief has given him clearance. We understand he hasn't completed the certification, but the director needs boots on the ground ASAP." He paused. "Paws as well."

"Where's the mission located?"

"Not too far from where you're at." Desmond paused again as if he was deciding whether to share the information over the phone.

Tanya waited, holding her breath.

Do they know what's going on in Paradise Cove?

For a moment, she wondered if she should tell him what she had seen. But after last night, she was sure her employer wouldn't approve of her clandestine activities.

Besides, there were protocols to follow.

Sheriff Reginald should be the one calling in, requesting help from the FBI. Federal and county officials worked well in teams. Coming down hard on local precincts stirred bad blood, and such efforts failed before they even began.

"I'll fill you in with the details when you come in," said Desmond. "See you then, Stone."

As soon as she hung up, a thrilling sensation rushed up Tanya's spine. She smiled to herself.

She had missed the adrenaline rush of embarking on new missions. Training flabby corporate executives on basic martial arts techniques at David's New York dojo hadn't been her dream job, however much she had been grateful for it.

It was exciting to know she'd be on the road again, even if it was only within this state.

She changed into her street clothes and stepped out of her bedroom, almost colliding with Asha.

"Boss just called," said Tanya.

Asha's face fell. "What do they want?"

"I have to get back on Tuesday."

Relief crossed her friend's face. "At least they didn't ask you to come in today. We still have a couple of days together to figure out what's going on in this town."

"First thing's first," said Tanya as she and Asha climbed down the stairs and walked into the open kitchen. "We need to tell the sheriff what we found last night."

"What if the deputies and the sheriff are dirty?"

"It's a risk we have to take. That would be a good reason to call my boss. Right now, there's nothing to get the FBI involved."

"What about those children on the murder board? Don't they fall under FBI jurisdiction?"

"Missing minors of tender years are a federal matter. That means twelve or younger."

"None of those kids looked twelve." Asha shook her head. "Couldn't the FBI make an exception for early teens? They're still children, aren't they?"

"I'd like to check the veracity of those pictures and names. For all we know, Eveline Hart was mentally disturbed or delusional. She could have photocopied those photos from random newspaper articles."

Asha opened the fridge door and reached for the orange juice. "I have a feeling this whole town knows what's going on except for us. Katy should call her foster mom. She might have an idea."

Tanya didn't respond.

Asha closed the fridge and looked up to see her friend staring at the kitchen window.

"What—"

"It's gone," said Tanya, opening the back door and stepping out. "Someone erased the message."

Asha padded over to the open door, the juice container still in her hand. "This is getting bizarre."

"How come I didn't hear them last night? I'm not a light sleeper." Tanya frowned. "This is why I need Max."

She peered at the flattened grass by the back window.

"They didn't leave footprints. I bet they used gloves too, so there would be no fingerprints either. They were careful to make sure we saw it before cleaning it up."

"We have a photo, at least," said Asha, taking out her phone.

"Send it to me." Tanya paused. "It's time I tell the sheriff I'm with the FBI."

"Oh, boy," said Asha.

It wasn't a conversation Tanya was looking forward to. The sheriff could throw them in jail, complain to the bureau, and stop her career before it even started.

"Are you two ready to go?" said Tanya, shaking off her worries. "Best to catch the sheriff while he's fresh."

"Katy's not feeling well," said Asha. "I think she was up all night, worried about that vase."

"That's the least of our problems right now."

"Let her sleep. Give her some rest."

Tanya scanned the backyard. "I don't like leaving her alone."

"I'll stay with her," said Asha.

"Keep all doors locked and don't go outside till I return."

"Anyone coming here looking for a fight with Katy and me will be making a big mistake."

"My Glock's on the bed stand in my room," said Tanya. "I could get fired for this, but I'm going to leave it with you, just in case."

"Thanks, but I don't think we'll need it," said Asha. "No one's going to break in in broad daylight."

Tanya picked up the Jeep's keys, hoping her friend was right.

Chapter Sixteen

Deputy Blake was leaning against his squad car, having a smoke, when Tanya pulled up at the sheriff's office.

He shot her a keen look, then threw his cigarette down and grounded it with his heel. He turned as if he was going to approach her.

I don't have time for you.

Ignoring him, Tanya marched toward the main entrance, her mind and heart racing. The idea of getting thrown in a county jail and having to call her boss made her sick to her stomach.

As soon as she flashed her FBI badge at the desk sergeant, he let her in through the secured doors. Tanya walked through the precinct's bullpen toward the largest office.

The back wall of the sheriff's office was lined with fishing photos.

They were all taken on a sleek white boat, a grinning Hudson Wyatt standing next to the sheriff in each of them, some with the fish they had caught, others with beer bottles in hand. There were other men in the background of the photos. They looked vaguely familiar, but their faces were blurred, so it was hard to make them out.

That must be Wyatt's famous yacht, she thought. She wondered how long he would be able to hang on to his toys once the family business's bankruptcy procedures went through.

She knocked.

Sheriff Reginald raised his head and frowned.

His eyes were bloodshot and his forehead was lined. A row of plastic coffee cups sat on his desk, in between piles of thick manila folders. The room felt stuffy and smelled like someone had left a stale bologna sandwich lying around for days.

For a brief second, Tanya felt for the man. He was just another overworked and under-resourced law enforcement officer with mountains of paperwork.

She stepped inside and closed the door.

"I'm an FBI agent."

Sheriff Reginald froze in place, one hand still holding his pen and the other, the document he had been reading.

Tanya took a chair from across his desk.

"I wanted you to know before you found out any other way."

She was about to use a negotiation tactic she'd learned at the bureau. When you find yourself at fault, confess quickly and early. That usually lessens the sting and preempts the other party from blaming you most of the time.

Unless the other party is a psychopath.

The sheriff frowned, but didn't speak.

Tanya leaned in.

"I owe you an apology."

He raised an eyebrow.

"I haven't been completely upfront with you."

The sheriff dropped his pen and paper on the desk. He reclined in his chair, folded his arms across his chest, and stared at Tanya, like he was sizing her up.

"I came here for a holiday with friends," said Tanya. "But like you, when someone's in trouble, I can't help but step in. That's the reason I jumped in when the SUV crashed into the café."

Silence.

"It's also why I did some further investigation."

The sheriff leaned forward and placed his arms on the desk.

"What do you mean *further investigation*?" he said, speaking slowly, a light flush crawling up his neck.

Tanya opened the app on her phone where she had stored the murder board photos. Then, she placed her cell on his desk.

"We found this last night."

The sheriff grabbed his eyeglasses and put them on before taking the device in his hands.

"Where did you find this?"

"In Eveline Hart's pantry."

He looked up. "What were you doing there?"

A blue vein on his neck was throbbing now. That wasn't good.

"My friends are private detectives. One of them came up with the brilliant idea to do some investigative work. When I went in search of her, I found her in Eveline Hart's house, where she had discovered this."

"How did you get into Eveline's house?"

Tanya wasn't going to answer that.

"I take full responsibility. My friend was only doing what she thought was the right thing."

"My guys locked everything up." The sheriff's frown deepened. "Besides, they were all over that house yesterday. They would have told me if they had found this."

"My friend found a false partition at the back of the pantry. It's not easy to figure out. Behind that is a hidden room where you will find this murder board with other evidence that might help you with the case."

"What else did you find?"

Tanya appraised him.

She could tell he was vacillating between the need to pry information and berate her. She was still unsure about him too, whether he was a clean or corrupt cop.

"We found a stack of family photos Eveline had been hiding. It's in a secret drawer behind a false vent in the kitchen wall. From those pictures, we believe the man in the truck was Eveline Hart's son. One of her sons."

"Eric Hart."

Tanya raised a brow. "So, you knew?"

The sheriff shifted his eyes. He was hiding something.

"Did you know him well?" said Tanya, keeping her tone and posture casual.

"He left town years ago, so I never met him, but we just got confirmation of the owner of the truck. They're running DNA tests and checking dental records to make sure, but it has to be him."

"Do you recognize any of the faces on the board?"

He shook his head. "They're so blurry. I'll get my guys to look at these."

"Who are these boys?" said the sheriff, as if speaking to himself. "And why was Eveline tracking them?"

"We think the kid at the end is a girl," said Tanya, watching him. "How many children have gone missing in this town, Sheriff?"

"None as far as I can recall. That's what's puzzling. These kids must all be from out of town."

He scrolled through the photos again and mumbled to himself.

Tanya peeked at her watch. She was getting antsy to return home. Leaving Asha and Katy alone bothered her, and more than ever now, she wished they had flown home the day before.

"Did Eveline have any law enforcement experience?" she asked.

"She was a local council member for as long as I can remember," said the sheriff. "Ran the PTA, was on the board of our farmer's market and non-profit charities."

"What about her husband?"

"Passed. Years ago."

"How did he die?"

"Heart attack. He dropped dead, just like that. Not even forty. Must have been stress." He shook his head. "A sad state of affairs for this family."

Tanya frowned. That was the second time she'd heard of a healthy man dying of a sudden heart attack at an early age. Then again, cardiovascular disease was the biggest killer in the country.

She pointed at her phone.

"Take a look at the photo of the second boy on the board."

The sheriff scrolled through the pictures.

"What about him?"

"We think it's a younger Jodie, the homeless kid who died in Pat's backyard yesterday. He was at the café, minutes before Eveline Hart's SUV crashed. I don't believe he died of an opioid overdose."

He stared at her. "Is that right?"

"There's a strong possibility Jodie was poisoned. If it were up to me, I would recommend an autopsy ASAP."

The sheriff picked up a coffee cup and sipped it, as if he was contemplating his next steps.

He was calm.

Too calm.

A nervous twitch started on Tanya's neck. She felt like she was waiting for the executioner's ax to fall.

She observed the sheriff discreetly. She had met enough criminals around the world to discern good from evil, but it was never easy and she had misjudged in the past.

Sheriff Reginald's eyes narrowed.

"So, it's Special Agent Stone, is it?"

Tanya didn't reply.

There was a glint in his eyes. It was a sinister look, one that Tanya had seen in power-hungry men—men who liked to have total control over their domain.

She braced herself.

"I'll make a deal with you," said the sheriff.

He's a dirty cop, after all.

"I won't complain to the bureau," he said, "and I won't charge your friends for trespassing in a crime scene or interfering in a murder investigation."

"In return?" said Tanya, her voice hardening.

"I want you to work for me."

"I already have a job."

"That's your problem."

Tanya clenched her jaws.

"You and your pals can't leave until you find out what the heck is going on in my town. For the record, this isn't a paid gig."

You psychopath.

"It will be good to have a federal agent working for me."

Tanya felt like someone had punched her in the stomach.

A leer broke across the sheriff's face, like he knew he had cornered his prey.

"I want you to report back on everything you find. No one in this town can know I'm on their tail."

Chapter Seventeen

It took Tanya twenty minutes to drive to the veterinarian's clinic.

Her mind buzzed with the conversation she'd had with Sheriff Reginald. She considered various scenarios and their consequences, and they all looked bleak.

Max was waiting for her in a kennel in the back, looking miserable. He licked her hand and wagged his tail, but his movements were lethargic. The way he looked at her with his woeful brown eyes made Tanya feel like the meanest human on earth.

After fussing over him and thanking the vet, she carried Max to the Jeep, her arms straining under his eighty-five pounds. Throughout the ride back to their home stay, he shifted his cone-covered head on the back seat and let out depressingly heavy sighs.

"You'll feel better soon, bud," Tanya said as she sped down the highway. "You'll be running around the woods chasing squirrels in a couple of days. I promise you."

Max raised his head and howled, the husky in him coming out. She could almost hear him say *how could you do this to me?*

"I know. I know. I'm the most horrible mom on earth. Sorry sweetie, but it had to be done. Bureau policy."

She glanced in the rearview mirror.

"We have a new case, bud. We'll be out of this hole and back on the road on a real FBI mission. You'll get to chase bad guys again. It will be fun."

Max lowered his head with another mournful sigh and closed his eyes. Tanya turned her attention back to the road.

She had been trying to forget her meeting with the sheriff, but it kept swirling in her head.

Power-hungry jerk.

A flash of anger swirled up her spine.

Most small-town cops were good, professional folk who just wanted to do their jobs. But there was always one wannabe Gestapo, seeking to assert their authority by any means necessary.

Sheriff Reginald was reveling that he had an FBI agent at his beck and call. He didn't know the only reason she had agreed was because she was on probation.

Tanya wanted to get to the bottom of this baffling crime too. If he had asked nicely, she would have offered her help. But now, she thought, gritting her teeth, he had only made an enemy of her.

She had forty-eight hours.

Forty-eight hours before her boss expected her at HQ in Seattle.

Forty-eight hours to uncover this town's secrets and find out if this psychopath sheriff had a hand in this crime too. If he was dirty, he would never go ahead with his threat and call the attention of the bureau.

I'm calling your bluff, Sheriff Reginald.

Tanya turned into Sunset Drive, her shoulders taut and face scrunched in anger.

You're going to regret bullying me.

She pulled up to their home stay's driveway and parked the Jeep.

Their street had fallen silent again. If she hadn't witnessed the gruesome murders the day before, she would have thought this was an idyllic community where rich people retired to lead uneventful lives.

When Tanya opened the back door to get Max, he had fallen asleep. She picked him up in her arms and carried him to the front door.

The door opened before she got within five feet of it.

"Oh, Max," said Asha, standing in the doorway. "You poor, poor boy."

"Can you move?" said Tanya, stepping up to the threshold. "He weighs as much as you."

Asha turned aside to let them pass, giving her the stink eye.

"For the record, I'm five pounds more than him."

Tanya smiled, knowing how her friend hated being reminded of her petite stature. She stepped around her and laid Max on the couch. Asha followed her in, waving a familiar piece of clothing in her hand.

Tanya frowned. "Where did you get that?"

Asha placed the torn blue hoodie on the coffee table. "Saw it at the bottom of the yard. I was just coming inside, when I heard you pull up."

"Didn't I tell you to keep all doors locked?"

"I was only gone five minutes. Katy's still sleeping upstairs. No one came inside."

Asha slipped her hand into the hoodie's pocket and withdrew a bank note.

"The hundred dollars I gave Jodie is still here. What does that say?"

"Did you find it on our yard or on Pat's side?"

"Our side." A look of alarm crossed Asha's face. "Maybe someone's trying to frame us."

Tanya grimaced as the conversation with the sheriff popped to her mind. "Right now, we can't trust anyone in this town."

She walked over to the front door and turned the bolt. She slipped the door chain in place and checked the handle to make sure it was locked. When she turned around, Asha was staring at something on the kitchen counter.

"Did you bring us breakfast?" said Asha.

"I didn't have time."

"Where did that come from, then?" Asha pointed at the plate of half a dozen muffins. A used paper wrapper lay next to a half-eaten muffin. "It wasn't there when I went to the yard."

"Didn't Katy say she was going to bake some for Pat today?" said Tanya.

"She changed her mind after she saw Pat snoop on us last night. Besides, she's still sleeping."

Max opened his eyes and twitched his ears, like he heard something. Tanya bent down to stroke his head. "Go back to sleep, bud. The doctor said you need to rest."

But he swiveled his head like he was searching for something, banging his cone on the back of the couch. He got on all fours and let the blanket fall from his back.

"What's up, bud?" said Tanya, her gut tightening.

"Carrot cake muffins," Asha was saying as she picked one up. "They're from Cora. She must have left it for us at the front door while I was gone. Katy already finished one."

Tanya walked over to the counter to see Cora's Corner Café emblem on the muffin plate. But something felt off.

The sound of a toilet flushing came from the second floor.

"Katy's up." Asha walked over to the staircase. "Hey, Katy? Come on down. Max is home and we have breakfast."

Max's ears perked. He jumped down from the couch and barked.

Tanya picked up the used wrapper and brushed the crumbles from it. A chill went down her spine.

"Asha!"

Asha came over to look. She read the words etched onto the silvery muffin wrapper.

Stop meddling.

Chapter Eighteen

A feeble voice called out from the second floor.

Max trotted toward the bottom of the staircase, barking.

"Katy?" said Asha, concern in her voice. "Are you okay, hun?"

Tanya whirled around. She raced up the stairs with Asha right behind her.

They got to the landing just as Katy stumbled out of the bathroom. She was still in her pajamas and looked woozy. She grabbed the railing and swayed, then fell to her knees. Tanya caught her just before she careened down the steps.

"Katy?" said Tanya, holding her head up. "What happened?"

"My s... stomach hurts," croaked Katy.

"Where did you find those muffins?" asked Asha.

"F... front... porch. I th... thought... it..."

Katy started trembling.

"I th... threw up."

She leaned against Tanya's shoulder, like she had no energy to hold her head up herself. Tanya checked her eyes and felt her pulse. Her breath was fast and raspy.

She spun around to Asha.

"We have to get her to a doctor ASAP."

Asha stared at her. "Cora tried to *poison* us?"

"Hurry!"

While Asha called for help, Tanya wiped the vomit residue from around Katy's mouth and checked her heart rate.

Though her face was pale and she was too feeble to talk, Katy's eyes were open. She was alert and knew what was going on, and that was good news.

"I... oh... I..." Katy gagged. "I'm gonna throw up!"

Tanya thrust her arms under her legs and carried her to the bathroom. She held Katy's head up as she vomited into the toilet bowl again.

"Whatever it is," said Tanya, rubbing Katy's back, "get it out of your system."

Tears rolled down Katy's cheeks.

"Gosh... I..."

"Shh... keep your energy. We'll get you to a doctor soon."

"Ambulance is coming!" Asha called out from the first floor.

"I'll bring her down."

Tanya carried Katy down the stairs, one step at a time. By the time she got to the bottom of the steps, the sirens echoed through their street.

"That was fast," said Asha, rushing to the front door and pulling it open. The emergency vehicle screeched to a halt in front of their driveway.

Tanya sat on the bottom step with Katy's head on her lap, waiting for the medics. The less she moved Katy until they confirmed her vitals, the better it would be.

Two paramedics rushed in with a stretcher and a first-aid kit. Tanya and Asha hovered over them anxiously as they strapped Katy down and administered oxygen.

"What happened?" said one medic.

"She ate half of one of these." Asha showed them the plate of muffins. "We think these have been poisoned."

His eyebrows shot up. "Substance?"

"No idea. Someone left this on our front porch this morning. She vomited as soon as she ate one. That's not a coincidence."

"Call the sheriff's office," said the second medic, picking one side of the stretcher. "We'll give them our report on our end."

The last thing Tanya wanted was to talk to Sheriff Reginald, but he needed to know the risks she and her friends were taking by staying in this town.

"I'm going with her," said Asha as the medics scurried down the front steps, carrying Katy toward the back of the ambulance. "I'll take the muffins to the hospital, so they can test them."

"I'm right behind you." Tanya grabbed her keys and whistled to Max.

He waddled over.

"You're a good boy. You knew something was wrong with Katy, didn't you?"

Max wagged his tail. While he was wobbly on his feet, Tanya knew he wouldn't want to be left out of the action. Given the day's events, she didn't want to leave him alone at home either.

She held the front door open for him and unlocked the Jeep using the remote. She was helping him into the back seat when she heard a man call out from behind her.

"Is your friend okay?"

Tanya spun around.

Hudson Wyatt was coming over, his enormous dog trailing behind him. The Great Dane sniffed the Jeep's tires, then trotted to the back seat and peeked in through the open door, tail wagging.

He looked eager to make a new friend, but Max growled. He wasn't in the mood to play. Tanya nuzzled the Great Dane aside and shut the Jeep's door.

She turned to Wyatt and looked him in the eye. "Someone tried to poison her."

Wyatt's brow knotted. *"What?* How?"

"We found a plate of Cora's carrot cake muffins on our front porch this morning." She paused, watching for any telltale signs of guilt or nervousness.

Hudson Wyatt gaped like a fish for a few seconds.

"That's peculiar. I just got a plate of carrot cake muffins from Cora too."

Chapter Nineteen

Wyatt gestured toward his house.

"Found a plate on the front porch when I came in from my morning walk with Milo."

"Was there a note?" said Tanya.

"Didn't see one."

"You didn't get sick?"

"I was about to sit down for breakfast when I heard the ambulance. I came out to check if you were okay before going back to have my tea. Good thing I didn't."

How convenient.

"Yesterday, my friend told you she was going to bake muffins for our neighbor. You were the only person she mentioned that to. Then, this morning we find a plate of muffins on our doorstep. Strange coincidence, don't you think?"

Wyatt made a face like he just bit into a lemon.

"Anyone could have left those muffins. I got some too."

I only have your word for it.

As if he read her mind, he whipped out his phone.

"I took a pic to send a thank-you note to Cora." He turned the screen toward her. "See? This is my porch."

"I'll call the sheriff and Cora," said Tanya. "I'd be interested to see what they have to say."

"I don't think it's Cora."

"How so?"

"She never lets anyone take her things outside the café premises, let alone bring them all the way here. Whoever did this, didn't know her routine."

"What does Cora use for house deliveries?"

"White cardboard boxes. That's what I get when I order cake." Wyatt shook his head. "You have this wrong. Cora has been part of our community for decades. She would never do anything like this. It was strange to find this by my front door."

Tanya was impatient to head to the hospital and find out how Katy was doing, but Wyatt was opening up. Whether he was lying or not, she was learning more about this strange town.

"Any idea who did this?" she asked.

Wyatt shrugged. "I see boxed delivery packages and envelopes all the time on front porches, but not open plates of food. Who does that, anyway?"

Tanya frowned.

"Did you see anybody on the street during your walk?"

He scrunched his forehead as if he was trying to recall. "Deputy Blake patrols this area and does a wellness check on his aunt every day. Saw his squad car circle by a few times."

"Let's hope he has a dash cam, or that he was paying special attention to who was on the street this morning."

Tanya opened the driver's door of the Jeep to get in.

"I have to go."

That was when Wyatt cried out.

99

"Oh, no!"

The Great Dane started barking, sensing Wyatt's distress. Max sat up in the back seat and growled. Tanya spun around.

Her eyes darted up and down the driveway.

What's going on now?

Wyatt put his hands on his head. "Someone's trying to poison the entire neighborhood!"

As if hearing the commotion, Pat's front door opened. She appeared at the threshold, her cane in hand.

"Pat!" cried Wyatt.

Ignoring him, she bent down and picked up something from her porch.

Tanya's heart beat a tick faster. *She got muffins too?*

Wyatt waved at her. "No! Pat, don't pick that up!"

Tanya strode up to the fence. "Put that down! It could have poison."

Pat scowled at her.

"Didn't I tell you squatters to go away?" she snarled.

"Pat!" called out Wyatt, racing down the driveway.

As if she hadn't heard him, Pat hobbled inside and slammed the door shut.

Wyatt stopped in his tracks and raised his hands as if he couldn't believe his eyes. He turned to Tanya.

Tanya shook her head. Pat had made it abundantly clear that she wouldn't have anything to do with her.

"*You* go talk to her. I have to go take care of my friend."

She jumped into her Jeep and turned the key. She glanced at her rearview mirror as she rolled out of the driveway to see Wyatt banging on Pat's door, with Milo barking at his heels.

What a crazy place.

Tanya activated her phone by voice and asked it to dial Asha.

"How's she doing?" she said before her friend could say hello.

"They just took her to intensive care. They're going to flush her system."

"Where are you?" said Tanya.

"Emergency waiting room."

"Hang on. I'll be there in ten."

She was about to end the call when a bright flash of light blinded her. A deafening roar came from somewhere beside her. Tanya hit the brakes and screeched to a halt.

The blast rocked the Jeep.

"Down, Max!" she shouted, covering her head with her hands.

Max flew across the backseat and hit the door panel. He whelped in pain.

For one disorienting minute, Tanya was crouching behind a desert dune. A sniper rifle was in her hand. Fighter jets roared overhead. Her team was screaming commands while firing at the enemy.

But it was Asha who was screaming on the phone.

"Tanya! What happened? Are you okay?"

Her heart pounding, Tanya raised her head to see what had hit her. Her eyes widened as she spotted Eveline Hart's house from across the street.

The entire structure had exploded.

Chapter Twenty

E veline's home was engulfed in flames.

Tanya spotted a figure by the front door of the house. *Someone's trying to get out!*

She leaped out of her Jeep and ran across the street. Behind her, locked in the backseat, Max barked nonstop.

An ominous gray smoke was gathering over the house. *Gas,* thought Tanya, as she dashed across the lawn. *Eveline had a gas stove.*

Tanya was halfway across the lawn when a second explosion rocked the house. Something large and heavy flew by her, almost hitting her.

She dove to the ground and threw her hands over her head.

A yell came from the front porch.

Tanya raised her head.

The person was trying to crawl out, but was being subdued by smoke.

She scrambled to her feet and dashed up the front steps, ignoring the scorching flames raging around the building. Her eyes stung and for one quick second, she was sure every cell in her body would melt.

Tanya grabbed the man by the arm. That was when she realized who it was.

Deputy Blake.

She dragged him down the stairs and onto the lawn. He stumbled onto the grass, clutching his chest, coughing a rough hacking cough.

"We need to get out of here!" she cried.

Tanya threw his arm around her shoulders and half-carried him toward the street. The roar of the fire behind them intensified, but she dared not look back.

"My car," croaked Blake, pointing a shaky finger.

She looked up to see a police vehicle parked a few cars down from her Jeep.

"Where's your partner?" said Tanya as they scrambled toward his vehicle. "Is anyone else inside the house?"

Blake convulsed from another cough attack.

"I... was alone...."

Tanya dragged him toward his car and settled him in the driver's seat.

She noticed a plastic water bottle on the passenger seat and picked it up. She twisted the cap and handed it to him. Blake grabbed it and gulped it down like he hadn't had water for days.

Panting hard, Tanya plucked her phone out of her pocket and dialed the emergency line.

"Fire," she barked at the dispatch. "Sunset Drive. Eveline Hart's residence."

When she hung up, Blake had reclined in his seat and closed his eyes. He was breathing heavily but was in much better condition than she had expected.

"What were you doing inside the house?" said Tanya.

"Sheriff said to do a check. I was on patrol today."

"See anything unusual?"

"Everything was the same as we left it, except for a broken vase in the kitchen."

He opened his eyes and squinted at Tanya.

A pang of guilt shot through her. She wondered how much of their conversation the sheriff had disclosed to his deputies.

"Was there anything inside that would have started this fire?" said Tanya, pushing the image of the vase to the back of her mind.

Blake rubbed his face. "It was crazy. One minute I was about to lock up and head out. The next minute, the whole darned place blew up."

He turned and stared at the house like he couldn't believe he escaped that inferno, alive.

Tanya raised a brow. He was breathing normally now and his color had returned. He had recovered fast.

She turned and glanced at the burning mansion, a hand shielding her face.

"You're one lucky man," she said. "Good thing you were by the door. Otherwise, you'd have blown to bits too."

The sound of emergency sirens came from the distance. Inside her car, Max was in a barking frenzy.

"Firefighters are on their way," said Tanya. "Hang tight. I have to check up on my dog."

Without waiting for him to answer, she marched over to her Jeep. She opened the back door, feeling bad for leaving Max behind to watch her run into danger by herself.

Despite the cumbersome cone around his head and the post-surgery drugs in his nerves, he seemed to want to get back into action. Max loved to work, and the treat at the end was just a bonus. That's what made German Shepherds great K9 dogs.

As soon as Tanya opened the door, Max leaped into her arms, whining and wagging his tail, like he hadn't seen her in years.

She let him out of the car and put her arms around him, while he licked her hands and arms. His cone banged on her face, but those scratches were a small price to pay to see her dog happy.

"Good boy," said Tanya, checking his head and body for bruises from their sudden stop. "Just got shocked a bit, eh? Me, too, bud. See, I'm fine, too."

"Tanya!"

She jumped back, startled. She swiveled her head, wondering where the disembodied electronic voice was coming from.

"Tanya! What the heck's going on? Talk to me! What happened?"

Asha.

Tanya scrambled to the front seat and picked up her phone that had fallen into the seat well.

"Hey, I'm good. Max is good." She paused for a second. "How's Katy?"

"Katy's still in the ops room. It's you I'm worried about." Asha's voice was partly angry, partly frightened. "I was just going to hang up when I heard the boom. Like a bomb went off. Then, you disappeared. I called nine-one-one. They said they were already going to the scene. Did you get into an accident? I told you to not use the phone while driving. Why don't you ever listen—"

"It wasn't an accident." Tanya lowered her voice. "That blast you heard was Eveline Hart's home blowing up."

Silence on the other end.

"Deputy Blake was by the door. I pulled him out, but he seems fine." Tanya looked up as three fire engines barreled down the street and halted by the burning house. "Fire trucks are here, but there's not much to salvage. It's all going up in flames."

Asha's voice came low and cautious. "Someone wanted to destroy the evidence."

"My thoughts, exactly."

"Good thing we took photos."

The firefighters scurried across Eveline's lawn, pulling heavy water hoses. Two squad cars raced over, lights flashing and sirens blaring.

"There's nothing we can do now," said Tanya. "I'll join you and Katy in a few minutes."

She hung up, wondering how the day could get any worse.

"There goes our property values."

Tanya whirled around.

It was Hudson Wyatt. He was standing a few feet behind her Jeep, hands in his pockets, a disappointed look on his face. His Great Dane was nowhere to be seen.

Tanya hadn't even heard him walk up.

A tapping sound made her peer over his shoulder. Pat was making her way toward them with her cane, wearing a grim expression on her face.

So Wyatt talked to her.

"I hope you didn't touch those muffins," said Tanya as she got closer.

Pat didn't answer, but stepped up to Wyatt on the curb. The two of them stood shoulder to shoulder, staring at the first responders trying to put out the fire in vain.

The roof was caving in and the house seemed to be imploding.

Wyatt shook his head. "How on earth does this sort of thing happen in Paradise Cove? This is such a peaceful town."

Pat let out an angry hiss.

Tanya watched her reaction in surprise.

Wyatt continued, seemingly oblivious to his neighbor's response.

"Nothing happens for decades, then all of a sudden, it seems like the entire town is blowing up."

"That could have been an accident," said Tanya, watching the two. "Or someone blew it up. Now, why would anyone want to do that?"

A pink flush crept up Pat's face. She pointed her cane at Eveline's home, her hand shaking.

"The demon house," she hissed.

Demon house?

Pat gave her a furious look. "This place should have been burned to the ground years ago."

Chapter Twenty-one

Without an explanation, Pat turned around.

She stomped back down the street, tapping her cane, heading toward her home. Tanya stared at her.

"Don't mind her," Wyatt said with a dismissive wave. "She can be trying some days."

Tanya stepped back toward her Jeep.

She didn't have time for these people or this town anymore. She had to take care of Katy first and get her friends away from this strange place. To hell with the sheriff and his power games.

She was about to jump in the driver's seat, when she realized something was missing.

No.

Someone.

"Hey, Max?"

She whirled around.

Where did he go?

"Max!"

She glanced at the fire, a sinking feeling coming to her stomach.

"Max, where are you?"

That was when she spotted his furry tail disappear by the cedar hedge that lined Eveline Hart's property. A flash of terror rushed through her.

"Max! Get back here!"

There was no way he would hear her over the chaos. Tanya leaped across the street, scooted around a fire truck, and ran toward the hedge.

"This area is closed off," shouted a firefighter, waving her away.

"My dog's back there."

He shot her a wild look.

"Can't you see the fire?"

"Bring the hose here, Jones!" came a sonorous voice.

The firefighter turned. "On it, Chief!"

Tanya didn't hang around.

Using her hand to shield her face from the heat, she slipped along the hedge and scuttled toward the back of the burning house. Debris and cinder were falling all over the place.

Max was bumbling along the edge of the woods, slower than usual, seemingly oblivious to the heat raging nearby. His nose was stuck to the ground like he had picked up a scent.

What's he doing?

"Max! Get back here!"

Behind her, Tanya heard another holler, but she didn't stop. She was about to cross the tree line and follow her dog in when she smelled the gasoline.

She stopped, her mind reeling.

Arson!

I knew it.

She scanned the area, expecting to see gas cannisters, but there were none. The arsonist had either taken the containers, or they were inside the crumbling house.

The fire crackled. Smaller explosions came as the structure keeled into itself. Tanya entered the woods just as the house came down in a thundering crash.

She leaped behind a pine tree. She looked out at the devastation, shocked to see a well-built mansion come down this fast.

Asha was right. Someone had wanted to get rid of the evidence Eveline had curated in her pantry.

Either they had planned this fire all along, or the sheriff had shared their photos with the culprit which had spurred this reaction.

An urgent bark made her spin around.

"Max?"

She wiped the sweat from her brow and surveyed the woods.

"Where are you, bud?"

She could hear rustling as he scampered through the underbrush.

Just before his operation, Max had completed a K9 search and rescue program, and something in this vicinity had triggered his nose.

"Max!" she hollered.

No answer.

Tanya weaved in between the massive tree trunks.

The sound of a twig breaking stopped her in her tracks. She scooted behind a tree, trying not to pant, listening. But the only sound she could hear was her own heart beating.

It was around noon, but it was dark among the trees. The heavy forest canopy kept the woods cool, a staggering contrast to the heat she had felt only moments earlier.

Tanya shivered.

She had no sense of how thick this grove was or how far Max had gone, but she had to find her dog and get to the hospital ASAP.

She plucked out her phone and clicked on the GPS. The app opened up, but the small circle in the middle turned round and round.

This is going to take forever.

She slipped her phone back in her pocket with a frustrated hiss and pulled her Glock out.

Max barked again, closer this time.

She stepped around the trees and peeked in between the leafy branches. She spotted his white cone bobbing up and down.

He was alone in a small clearing.

Around him, the trees had fallen silent. Even the birds seemed to stop chirping. It was an eerie spot.

After scanning the area to ensure no one else was nearby, she stepped out from behind the thicket and treaded over.

"What are you doing here, bud?" she whispered.

Max wagged his tail as if to say *it's about time you came.*

Tanya kneeled next to him, hitched her fingers around his collar, and looked him in the eyes.

"Don't you dare run off like that on me again, okay?"

He sneezed, as if to say sorry.

Tanya softened her voice. "Wait till I give the command, bud. If you do this again, I'll have to send you back to police dog school."

He turned and barked.

She stroked his back. He was trying to tell her something.

But what?

Her eyes swept the area. She surveyed the circle of fir trees. They looked like stern sentinels protecting the clearing.

It took her a few seconds to realize someone had set up a rough lean-to shelter in between the trees, about five yards from the clearing. It had been camouflaged by branches, sticks, and clumps of leaves. It was so well hidden, she wouldn't have noticed it if Max hadn't been barking in its direction.

Tanya got to her feet, gripping her Glock.

The shelter was large enough to fit a squatting adult, but too low to stand up in. There seemed to be an entrance of some sort on the side.

"Stay here," she whispered to Max.

She walked over, stopping every few steps to listen, her weapon at the ready in case something or someone jumped on her.

She was two yards from the shelter when she heard a bizarre sound.

Goose bumps sprang on her arms.

At first she thought it was kittens mewling. Then, she realized it was the sound of someone crying. Whoever it was stopped, as if they realized a stranger was listening from the outside.

Tanya pulled out her phone and turned on the flashlight.

"Hello? Anyone in there?"

Chapter Twenty-two

T anya stepped closer to the makeshift shelter.

The odor of unwashed homelessness wafted over to her, like Jodie had smelled when he'd brushed passed her at Cora's Corner Café.

She pushed the leafy branches out of the way, got to her knees, and peeked inside.

"Please don't hurt me," said a small voice.

It was almost pitch black, but she could make the outline of a child crouching in the far corner.

She shone her flashlight inside.

It was a boy.

No, it was a girl. And she looked vaguely familiar.

She was frail and about fourteen years old. She was huddled in the corner, hugging herself, and shaking so hard, her teeth chattered.

"Hey," said Tanya in her softest voice. "I won't hurt you."

She turned her flashlight away, so it wasn't shining on her face like an angry spotlight.

The girl didn't look up, still trembling. She looked more like a victim of famine from a faraway place, than a kid from anywhere near this upscale suburb.

Tanya holstered her weapon and turned her palms upward, to show that she wasn't a threat.

"My name is Tanya. What's yours?"

Silence.

Tanya inched toward the entrance on her knees. If she had to guess, the kid had been hiding here for a few days.

Tanya knew why children ran away from home and tried to survive on the streets. Or, in the woods.

Katy and Asha had been orphans when she met them a long time ago, when she was barely an adult herself. They had been lost kids, like herself, running away from abuse and horror.

Tanya leaned in. "What are you doing here, hun?"

The kid didn't answer. She didn't even look up.

Tanya racked her brain, trying to think of what she could say to make her engage.

The child needed food, water, a good cleanup, and medical attention. But it would take a miracle to coax her out of this rancid refuge and into a safe place.

"Are you hungry?"

The girl turned to her, tears filling her eyes.

Tanya felt in her jacket pockets, then rummaged through her cargo pants, hoping she had a protein bar or even a piece of candy. But all she had on her was her wallet, keys, phone, Swiss army knife, and her Glock.

"If you come with me," she said. "I can get you a nice hot meal. How does that sound?"

The kid stared at her, a veil of suspicion coming over her eyes.

"There's an extra room in my house. It has a nice bed, a bathroom, and even a TV. You can come over and wash up, while I make a grilled cheese sandwich for you. It's cozy inside, too. Would you like that?"

The girl didn't answer, but a twitch came on her mouth.

"It's not too far from here," said Tanya. "Just a few minutes' walk up the road to Sunset Drive."

The girl's shoulders stiffened. She pulled in her legs and hugged her knees.

Tanya's brow knotted. "Did you used to live on Sunset Drive?"

The kid crumpled into a ball, looking even more scared now.

"Where's your family, hun?"

Silence.

"I know a few people on Sunset Drive," said Tanya, keeping her voice casual and friendly. "There's Eveline Hart. Do you know her?"

The child shot her a furtive glance from under her lashes.

She knows, but she's not telling. Why?

"There's Hudson Wyatt. He owns a great big dog and has a nice green car. How about him?"

The kid flinched, but didn't reply.

So, she knows the man in the fancy suit too.

"There's Pat." Tanya paused. "I don't know her last name, but she walks with a cane."

The girl shuddered and hugged herself closer.

"Do you know her? Would you like me to take you to her?"

"No!"

The girl gave her such a terrified look that Tanya leaned away.

They sat in silence for a minute. *She's traumatized,* thought Tanya as she watched the kid. *What on earth happened to her?*

Tanya's heart ached to see the girl living like a feral animal. Even after experiencing the horrors of war in some of the darkest corners of earth, it was painful to see a child in such misery.

"Don't worry. We don't have to see anyone on Sunset Drive. To tell you the truth, I don't even know any of these people."

"Please don't hurt me."

"Hun, were there other kids with you?"

The girl nodded.

Tanya leaned closer. "Do you know Jodie?"

The kid froze, then gave a barely perceptible nod.

Tanya sat up. "When was the last time you saw him?"

The girl shrugged. "He went to get food."

Tanya closed her eyes.

Those sugar buns. These poor kids.

"Are you and Jodie running away from someone?"

The girl gave another brief nod, but wasn't looking at Tanya anymore. Her heart fell as she realized the girl didn't know about Jodie's death. There would be a time to tell her, but now was not that time.

She tried to recall the other names on the list.

"What about the others? Do you know Liam, Matt, and Peter?"

The girl didn't answer, but the question seemed to trouble her even more. She rocked back and forth, her eyes downcast, pretending to examine her toes. But Tanya knew she was only trying to avoid looking at her.

The kid rubbed her foot and mumbled to herself.

That was when Tanya saw it.

She turned her flashlight onto the girl's hand and the hair on the back of her neck rose.

This girl had been branded with the same heart-shaped mark as Jodie had been.

116

Chapter Twenty-three

A rustle came from behind Tanya.

She whipped around, one hand on her holster.

It was Max. He had moved closer, as if he had wanted to ask what was taking so long. Tanya suddenly realized what she had on her.

"Hey, Max," she called out. "Come over here, bud."

He trotted over and sniffed the makeshift shelter.

"Good boy."

She stroked his back and nudged him down, so he would face the opening. Max pushed his coned head between Tanya and the entrance and settled down. He lowered his head between his paws and let out a loud sigh.

The girl turned toward the dog. Max wagged his tail twice. The girl's eyes widened. She didn't move but her shoulders seemed to relax.

Max was the miracle Tanya had been looking for.

"My pup found you," she said. "He came looking for you because he knew you needed help."

The girl didn't look at her, but pushed a hesitant hand close to the dog, as if she was deciding whether to touch him. Max shuffled a few inches closer and stuck his snout inside. The kid reached his nose. Max licked her hand.

The girl's face scrunched up, like she was about to cry. Tanya wondered if this was the first time anyone had made physical contact with her in a long time.

"He's trained to protect people." Tanya paused. "His name is Max. What's yours, hun?"

"Noel."

Her voice had quavered, but Tanya knew she had heard it right. That name had been on the list. This was the kid who had looked like a boy at the end of the row of photos. The one with the aquamarine beaded choker.

"Noel?" said Tanya with a smile. "That's a beautiful name. It's really nice to meet you, Noel."

The girl kept her eyes downcast.

"Hey, Noel, how old are you?"

She shrugged.

"Seventeen," she whispered. "I think."

A shiver went through Tanya. *She looks barely fifteen.*

"Did somebody take you from your home a long time ago?"

Noel nodded.

"How old were you when they took you?"

Another shrug. "Thirteen. I think."

Tanya leaned back with a heavy heart. The girl didn't need just medical attention, she needed someone to help her and emotionally recover from whatever hell she had gone through.

The girl reached over and touched the top of Max's head. She was getting bolder.

"When was the last time you ate a good meal, Noel?"

The girl turned to her, hope coming to her eyes.

She was hungry.

"See Max, here? He's starved too. He'd like it if you came with him. There's a grilled cheese sandwich waiting for you if you do."

The girl's eyes were quizzical but not as apprehensive as before.

"I promise you, I'll take you to a safe place."

The girl looked at Max, then at her. Then, to Tanya's surprise, she bent down and got on all fours, as if she was about to crawl out.

Tanya backed away and whistled for Max to pull out. She moved toward the nearest tree and leaned against the base, like she had all the time in the world.

She had been trying to get to the hospital for more than an hour now. She was dying to call Asha, but didn't dare in case the kid got scared and ran off.

She plucked her phone out and swiped to the image of the murder board. It was hard to say how long ago these photographs had been taken, and Noel now looked malnourished, but she zoomed in on the photo at the end.

Her heart skipped a beat.

She knew for sure now. She had found another of the lost kids.

Tanya squatted by the tree for an agonizing ten minutes before the girl decided it was safe to leave her hideout. Just when Tanya thought she'd have to try another persuasion tactic, Noel poked her head out and blinked.

The girl extricated herself inch by inch, her shoulders drawn, and her back hunched. Then, she sat in front of the shelter and glanced around her, like she expected a tiger to pounce on her.

Max took position next to her, as if guarding her. Tanya watched the girl, sizing her up.

She was skin and bone, and shivering.

Tanya took off her jacket and pushed it toward her. The girl took it and placed it around her shoulders.

Tanya settled back against her tree and smiled.

"We can get that grilled cheese sandwich whenever you're ready."

"I'm hungry."

The girl was staring at her, her eyes moist. She had her hand out, like she was begging.

Tanya felt something in the pit of her stomach. Then, an angry ball of fire raced up her spine.

Whoever did this to this girl is going to pay.

Tanya got on her haunches and reached over to touch the girl's hand. This time, she didn't pull back.

"Come with me," she whispered.

The girl was so weak, she had a hard time standing. She grabbed onto Tanya's arm with one hand and clutched Max's collar with the other.

Tanya sent her pup a silent thanks, glad he had finished the most important part of his training. He knew when to attack and he knew when to remain calm.

She smiled at the girl. "Let's go get that sandwich for you and some kibbles for Max."

Noel stumbled along, flanked by her and Max.

The fastest path back to their house would be through Eveline Hart's backyard, but that would be the most dangerous route. There were too many people and one of them could be the person who had harmed this kid.

Though it would take longer, Tanya led her deeper into the woods, walking in the general direction of their home stay. They were lucky the Harts' residence was on the same side of the street as theirs.

Given Noel's slow and hesitant pace, it took them a while to get to the edge of their backyard. That was when Tanya realized the risk she was taking. Anyone looking their way would spot the girl.

Tanya could feel Noel was getting weaker, leaning unsteadily on her arm. She had no choice.

She scanned the homes on both sides. They looked empty, but she knew anybody could be peeking from the corner of those windows.

She pulled out the house keys Katy had given her and put an arm around the girl's shoulder. She whispered in her ears.

"Hold on tight. I'm going to carry you and run. Ready?"

Without waiting for her to reply, she put her arms under her knees, picked her up, and sprinted toward the back of their house.

The closest entrance was the one to the sunken basement suite.

Tanya tried the house keys, one by one, mentally crossing her fingers. To her relief, the second key fit. She unlocked the door and pushed Noel inside.

While Noel sat at the edge of the bed, blinking, disoriented, Tanya walked about the suite, drawing the curtains.

She got to the last window when she spotted a dark silhouette by the kitchen window of the neighbor's house.

Pat!

Tanya pulled the curtain across.

Did she see Noel?

Chapter Twenty-four

"How's Katy?"

"Much better," came Asha's voice down the line. Tanya leaned against the kitchen counter and sighed in relief.

"They flushed the toxicity out of her system and are monitoring her for adverse reactions," said Asha. "She's awake and talking, but weak."

"What's their diagnosis?"

"She was poisoned for sure. The doctor said it's a good thing she only took a few bites and threw up soon after. If she had eaten a whole muffin and let it digest, she'd probably be in awful shape."

"She's going to be okay, right?"

"She needs to rest. She's only allowed black tea and crackers for the next couple of days. She's already complaining about missing her morning caramel lattes and cake treats. That's going to be tough on her."

"If that's all she's griping about, she'll be fine," said Tanya, relief flooding through her. "Do they know what made her sick?"

"They think it's brodifacoum."

"*Rat poison?*"

"They're testing the muffins, but there's a backlog. Lab results won't be out for another forty-eight hours. That's if we're lucky."

"Do they know two more homes had these cakes left on their doorsteps?"

"A deputy from the sheriff's office came to take a statement about an hour ago," said Asha. "He didn't seem overly interested but said they'll check on it."

"Did you share the wrapper with the note?"

"I handed it to him, but I got the impression he would have taken things more seriously if Katy had died."

Tanya winced.

"He looked like a rookie to me. Didn't even bother to bag the wrapper. I think you should take over this team. Teach them some basic skills."

Asha paused.

"I called Cora and thanked her for the muffins. She seemed genuinely confused. I don't think it was her. Someone was trying to frame her."

"We don't want to jump to conclusions," said Tanya. "How long are they going to keep Katy in the hospital?"

"They will discharge her this afternoon. The paperwork might take a while. Can you pick us up in a couple of hours?"

Tanya lifted her head and peeked into the living room.

Noel was on the couch next to Max, huddled under a blanket. With Tanya's help, she had showered and changed into a clean pair of shorts and T-shirt Tanya had dug out of the basement closet.

She now held a grilled cheese sandwich in one hand and was clutching onto Max's collar with the other, like she was scared he'd leave her.

Tanya had picked out a can of vegetable broth from the pantry which would have been much more kind to Noel's malnourished body, but she had chosen the sandwich instead. She hoped she wouldn't get sick.

Tanya had locked all the doors and windows, and drawn all the curtains in the house. She had turned on the TV to a cartoon channel and handed the girl the remote, but she hadn't touched it and had been staring blankly at the screen. Her eyes didn't waver during commercials and she didn't laugh at the jokes.

Tanya wondered what was going through her head.

She turned back to her phone. "Some pretty crazy stuff have been happening here."

"I'm glad that blast didn't get you and Max," said Asha. "Did they save Eveline Hart's house?"

"Nothing will be left but ashes."

Asha tsked.

"I took another look at the photos," she said. "It kept me busy while they were taking care of Katy. I went through the paper clippings, the pictures, and the list of names and dates." She paused. "This is a wild guess, but think I know who those men on the board are."

Tanya straightened up.

Asha lowered her voice. "They—"

"Asha," said Tanya, stopping her friend. "I have a small urgent thing to get to right now. Why don't we chat some more when you come home, okay?"

She knew how easily cellular signals could be picked up. She doubted a small town like this would have anyone with the technological knowhow or the tools to hack their call, but she couldn't take the risk.

When Asha's voice came again, it was low and cautious. "See you in a few hours, then?"

Tanya glanced over at Noel again. Given what had happened to Jodie, taking Noel outside could mean certain death to her too. At the same time, she didn't wish to leave her alone.

"My hands are tied," she said. "I can't come right now."

"No worries. I've got this."

"Catch a rideshare or taxi as soon as they discharge Katy. Don't hang around and don't stop on your way."

"Understood," said Asha.

Tanya's phone buzzed as a second call came in.

She stared at the name crawling across her screen. Sheriff Reginald was the last person she wanted to talk to. She ignored the call and said goodbye to Asha before hanging up. She was about to join the girl when her phone buzzed again.

What does he want?

Tanya let the phone ring.

Let him wait.

The ringing stopped but started again almost instantly. This time, she accepted the call.

"Yes?"

"Stone," said Sheriff Reginald. "You got your police dog with you?"

"What do you want with him?"

"I could do with a K9 to sniff around the fire incident for body pieces, clues, and such."

Tanya narrowed her eyes.

"My dog isn't going anywhere near that scene."

"Why not? The fire's out."

"They may have doused the flames, but the temperature will be too high. Last time I saw that property, it was crumbling in pieces. The area is unsafe."

"My boys tell me they saw your dog in the backyard when the fire was raging. Seems like he's a hardy pup. Bring him over. I need him."

Tanya closed her eyes and let out a frustrated hiss.

"He doesn't work for you."

"*You* work for me." The sheriff's voice hardened. "Did you forget our agreement, Stone?"

She thought of the many words she'd like to fling at him, but knew that wouldn't help her.

"My dog's not coming anywhere near that scene until the fire chief gives the all-clear."

Before he could reply, she hung up, and threw the phone on the counter.

Tanya stepped into the living room. She walked over to the couch and kneeled on the floor next to Noel, who was stroking Max's back.

"How are you doing?" she said, softening her voice.

Noel gave her a blank look, then turned back to the TV.

"Is your family from Paradise Cove?"

Silence.

"Do you have a family name? Can you tell me your mom or dad's names, hun?"

"I don't have any."

"How about sisters or brothers? Uncles or aunts, maybe?"

Noel shrugged, then hung her head.

"I grew up at the foster center."

A chill went down Tanya's back.

Traffickers were known to prey on abandoned or runaway children. They were the easiest to groom and least likely to be reported missing. Had Noel been a ward of the state?

Tanya wanted to ask her what happened during the past three or so years, but she wasn't the right person to coach anyone through trauma. They had Harvard-trained psychologists in the bureau for this.

She knew all too well how badly past nightmares could haunt you, if they weren't taken care of by professionals.

She leaned over.

"Can you tell me who took you, hun?"

Noel didn't reply, her eyes on her half-eaten sandwich now.

Tanya was about to ask again, when Max turned his head, the cone scraping the girl's hand. Noel jerked back, startled.

Max got up, leaped down from the couch and trotted to the front door, a stern expression on his face.

Tanya jumped to her feet.

"What is it, bud?"

Max growled.

Is someone on the other side?

Chapter Twenty-five

The handle on the front door dipped and sprang up.

Someone was trying to get in.

Max let out a volley of barks. Tanya marched over, her heart racing.

"Hey, Stone?" called out Blake from the other side. "Can we talk?"

Tanya peeked through the peephole to see the deputy she had pulled out from the burning house now in front of their door. He looked in perfect health, like he hadn't been doubled over, hacking and coughing only an hour ago.

She turned around and walked back to the couch.

"Noel, I want you to go to your room," she whispered. "Lock your door and don't come out until I tell you to."

Noel stared at her, mute and immobile.

A bang on the door made her jump.

"Open up, please! This is urgent."

Max barked back in reply.

"There's a TV downstairs," whispered Tanya. "You can eat your sandwich and watch it from there. It's more cozy in your room."

The banging came on the front door again, louder.

Noel sat up, as if she suddenly realized what was going on. She picked up her plate and got to her feet. Tanya took her by the arm and hurried toward the door that led to the basement staircase.

She helped Noel down the steps, thankful the basement was a fully equipped suite with a toilet and a mini kitchen. If she had to confine the girl in there until she figured out what to do next, she would at least be comfortable.

"Don't open the curtains, windows, or the doors," whispered Tanya. "Promise?"

Noel gave her a frightened nod before scooting over to the bed.

"I want you to stay here till I come back. Don't open the door to anyone but me, okay?"

To Tanya's surprise, Noel lifted her hand as if to acknowledge her. Tanya wished she could give her a hug, but worried how the girl would react. She waved back, locked the basement door from the inside, and pulled it shut.

Max was barking his head off upstairs.

She ran up the steps and stomped over to the front door.

"Hang on!" she hollered and flung the door open.

Max lunged forward.

Deputy Blake sprang back in alarm. He stumbled and fell down the steps.

"What do you want?" snapped Tanya, making no move to stop Max who was barking, inches from the deputy's knees.

Blake crouched on the bottom step, his shoulders scrunched, and his hands shielding his face.

"Call him off!"

"I asked a question," said Tanya.

"The sheriff.... Sheriff Reginald wants you to come with your dog. Said it was urgent."

A swirl of anger spiraled up Tanya's spine.

Who do they think they are to order me around like this?

"You can tell him my dog doesn't work for him."

She whistled to Max. Still growling, Max turned around and trotted up the steps toward her. She closed the door halfway when Blake hollered.

"I need to talk to you!"

Tanya looked at the deputy in surprise.

Blake got up and shot a worried look over his shoulder, as if expecting to see an angry sheriff. He turned back to Tanya with pleading eyes.

"Can I come in?"

"Not a chance."

"There's something I need to tell you."

Blake's eyes flitted like he was trying to choose the right words.

Tanya watched him, wondering what triggered this hundred-and-eighty-degree change.

This was the man who had arrested her without cause, lied to his boss about the scar on the dead man's hand, and had been at the house when the fire started. There was something off about his behavior.

"Sheriff said you were a vet." He paused awkwardly. "Thank you for your service."

Tanya stared at him, unsure if he was mocking her.

Blake rustled up a gawky smile. "I, er... really wanted to thank you for saving my life."

Tanya stood in stony silence.

"I mean it," said Blake, seeing her face. "You risked your life to get me out of that burning building. I wanted to say a sincere thank you."

Tanya pushed on the door to close it.

Blake put a hand on the door.

"Please! Hear me out."

"Get your hands off my door."

He pulled back.

"This... this... this isn't easy for me to say," he stammered. "I'm sorry, I, er, arrested you at the crash site. I know you were trying to stop Eveline Hart from shooting her son." He paused. "Look, er, why don't you come and talk to the boss. It shouldn't take a minute. He's going to make a hell of a fuss if you don't."

"Your problem, not mine, Deputy."

Footsteps made her look up.

Blake's partner was coming up the driveway now, and another officer was making his way down the street. It seemed like Sheriff Reginald was sending his troops to convince her.

Tanya put her hands on her hips and glared at the officers lining up on the driveway.

"We got off in the wrong footing." Blake spread his hands. "We're on the same side."

Great, thought Tanya, this is exactly what I need. A crew of deputies at the front door while that scared little girl sat in the basement, hearing the commotion and wondering what was going on.

She picked up Max's leash from the side table and stepped out, whistling to him to follow her out. She locked the front door and double-checked it, hoping Noel remembered her instructions to lie low.

"Ten minutes," she barked to the deputies. "We'll walk around the perimeter, but neither I nor my dog are going anywhere near the debris. His safety is paramount. Understood?"

"Sure thing," said Blake, a look of relief coming over his face. "That's perfect. It will satisfy the sheriff."

Tanya stomped down the steps with Max at her heels.

"You don't have a sheriff in this town," she said to the men flanking her. "You have a Nazi Gestapo."

Neither officer replied, but their faces told her she had hit close to the truth.

"Is he from Paradise Cove?"

"His wife's from here," said Blake in a quiet voice. "Her family owns a lumber mill. Largest in the county."

The fishing photos lining the sheriff's office wall flashed across Tanya's mind. This explained why the sheriff went fishing on Hudson Wyatt's yacht. They were brothers-in-law.

"Powerful family?" she said.

The officers nodded.

"The sheriff uses it to his advantage, does he?"

No answer.

"Is the sheriff a fishing aficionado?"

"Sure is," said Blake.

"Hangs out on Wyatt's yacht?"

"Almost every weekend."

"What else does he do in his spare time?"

The cops shrugged.

"Hiking, fishing, boating," said Blake. "What everyone does around here."

Tanya could see Eveline Hart's house now. Or what was left of it.

The acrid smell of burning wood and plastic lingered in the air, stinging her nose. The firefighters had contained the flames, and were dousing the remnants of the structure with water. A handful of responders leaned against the fire trucks, clutching plastic bottles and wiping their soot-covered faces with towels.

Pat and Wyatt were nowhere to be seen, but a small crowd of onlookers had gathered along the street where they had been before. A few people looked up curiously to see what she and Max were doing with the deputies.

Tanya turned to the men, keeping her face stoic.

"Does the sheriff ever go to the back woods to hike or hunt?"

Blake gave her a startled glance, but before he could answer she heard someone holler.

"Stone!"

Sheriff Reginald was leaning against his squad car and waving at her like she was his new best friend.

"It's great to have a trained K9 in town." He grinned. "Thanks for volunteering, Stone."

Chapter Twenty-six

T anya gritted her teeth.

Voluntold, you mean?

"I'll start on the west end," she said in a gruff voice.

She turned away from the gloating sheriff.

If I'm going to do this, I'm doing it my way.

Without waiting for him to reply, Tanya guided Max toward the cedar hedge. She kneeled down and felt the grass. It was cool to the touch, suitable for Max to walk on.

She turned to face the ruins where gray smoke was rising. They were about forty yards from where the house had stood. The caustic smell of sulfur pervaded the area. She sniffed the air for gasoline, but it seemed to have evaporated.

Tanya led Max along the hedge, tracing their earlier path toward the back, while it seemed the entire town watched. She stepped carefully, eyes on the lawn, staying away from anything that looked like fire debris.

Max walked beside her on his leash, his nose to the ground. He was following her, not leading her, which told her there weren't any clues to uncover. She doubted there were any bodies in the rubble.

Tanya clenched her jaws. She was wasting her time just so the sheriff could look important.

She had been puzzling over why he was forcing her to work for him. If he was guilty of any crime, he would have wanted the FBI agent to leave town as quickly as possible.

She now had a theory for what drove his obnoxious personality.

If he felt insecure next to a wife who was the CEO of one of the largest companies in the state, she could see why he would assert his power over his small dominion.

Tanya had met men like him before, especially those who hadn't come to terms with modern society. She wondered why a smart woman like his wife would put up with a man like this. Then again, narcissistic people always knew on which side their bread was buttered.

Max stopped and turned his head as a noise came from behind. Tanya spun around to see Deputy Blake scurrying over.

Go away, she hissed under her breath.

She pulled on Max's leash and picked up her pace, hoping it would deter him. She was sure the sheriff sent him to monitor her, and she didn't need an annoying tail.

The deputy ran up.

"Find anything?"

Tanya grunted in reply.

"My boss is super impressed with your work." He fell in step with her. "He said we could learn a few things from you."

Tanya gave him a discreet glance. He was lying.

Blake had a fresh face that made him look younger than he was. She couldn't help but feel like behind that pretty boy face, he was hiding something.

She turned to him. "What do *you* think happened here?"

"There were two five-hundred-gallon propane tanks behind the house." Blake pointed at the ruins. "They were for the kitchen appliances and for use as backups during blackouts. They malfunctioned and blew up."

"You think this was an accident?"

"Absolutely."

"I disagree."

Blake gave her a startled look.

"You're considering arson?" He shook his head as if he couldn't believe it. "That's impossible. Besides, Mrs. Hart died.... killed herself. There's no motive."

Isn't there?

"You know this town better than I do, Deputy," said Tanya, observing him. "Who could do something like this?"

"Beats me." Blake spread his hands. "This has to be an accident."

"Just like Jodie's death was an accident?" said Tanya.

Blake flinched but didn't reply.

"You were inside the house when the fire started," said Tanya. "Did you notice anyone sneaking around the back?"

"If I'd seen someone, I would have called it in. I saw nothing. I heard nothing. I opened the front door and *kaboom*. It blew up. Just like that."

Just like that, eh?

The more she thought about it, the more she wondered what Blake was doing in the house just before it exploded. He had recovered remarkably well and was back on the job, only a couple of hours after he looked like a victim of smoke inhalation.

From the corner of her eyes, Tanya caught sight of a taxicab crawling up the street. She turned and peered, but she couldn't make out who was inside the cab.

"So, what were you doing in the military?" Blake was saying. "Army, Navy, or Marines?"

Tanya gave him a quizzical look. So the sheriff hadn't told his crew she was an FBI agent?

"Special Forces."

"Wow. Respect."

"Retired," said Tanya.

Her gut had tightened.

Something told her Blake hadn't come to chitchat, or to thank her for saving his life, or to watch her for the sheriff. He was digging for information. Either that, or he was delaying her.

She whistled to Max and hurried along the property line, anxious to return to the house. If Asha and Katy had been in that taxi, they would soon find out there was a stranger in the basement. She couldn't say how Noel would react to see them.

"Now I know why you jumped in to stop Eveline and her son," said Blake. "I feel like an idiot for cuffing you." He gave her a sheepish grin. "Hey, can I buy you a drink? It's the least I can do for making a mess of things."

Tanya raised an eyebrow.

"There's a real nice drinking hole a block from Cora's Corner Café." Blake blushed. "I er, think you'll like it."

Are you asking me on a date, Deputy?

The taxi had stopped in front of their house now. Without giving Blake an answer, Tanya stepped back onto the street where the firetrucks were parked.

"Stone?" boomed a male voice.

The sheriff was strolling over, his fingers looped in his belt, his shoulders squared, as if to show everyone watching that he was in charge.

"Your dog find anything?"

"Nothing pertinent."

Tanya paused, trying to think of the fastest way to get away from him.

"I can come back once the fire chief gives the go-ahead. I'll get Max to sniff among the debris and see if there's anything he can find in there."

The sheriff nodded.

"Good thinking," he said. "Come in to the office. I have some files I need you to look into." He winked and clicked his tongue. "Might as well get some work out of you while you're in town, eh?"

Tanya's stomach tightened.

"No."

The sheriff's eyebrows shot up.

"What do you mean, *no?*"

"I mean, *no.*"

What the heck else does he think I mean?

Tanya took a breath in and let it out. "My friend was poisoned this morning. Before I do anything else, I need to check up on her—"

"Help!"

Everyone swiveled around.

It was Asha. She was racing down the street, waving at the firefighters. She halted by the fire truck, panting.

"Medical emergency! Someone's hurt!"

Tanya stomach sank.

Katy!

A responder plucked a medic's bag from the back of the nearest truck.

"Where?" he said.

Asha pointed at their home stay. "In our house. Hurry!"

Tanya pulled on Max's leash. "Let's go!"

Asha turned to her, her eyes wide. "There's a little girl in our living room. Someone tried to kill her!"

Noel!

Chapter Twenty-seven

Tanya let Max's leash fall to the ground.

"Go, Max!" she shouted, as she raced toward their home stay.

He bolted ahead of her and darted up the steps to where Katy was standing on the front porch.

She was holding on to the banister, her face pale, still not recovered from her ordeal. She waved to Tanya.

"Come! Hurry!"

Tanya whisked past her and burst into the living room.

She stopped as she saw the sight.

Noel lay motionless on her stomach, sprawled on the living-room floor. Her neck had bruise marks, like someone had choked her. Max was circling her, whining and nudging her as if to say *wake up*.

Her heart pounding, Tanya fell to her knees and put a trembling hand on Noel's neck.

Please be alive.

Her body was still warm to the touch. Tanya's heart leaped as she felt a faint pulse.

"Noel!" she called out, her voice cracking. "Stay with me. Can you hear me? Noel?"

The girl moaned.

A first responder dashed through the front door, slammed down his medic bag, and shoved Tanya to the side.

"CPR!" she hollered. "She needs—"

"Stay back, ma'am. We know what we're doing."

Tanya had trained in first-aid, but she knew she had to step away, realizing they were better equipped to take care of the child right now. She was shaking from shock and anger.

If Noel dies, she thought, blinking tears from her eyes, *I will put a bullet through the person who did this.*

"Who's this kid?"

Tanya looked up to see Asha walk over, a perplexed expression on her face.

"Did you get a look at the culprit?" said Tanya.

"I thought I heard something when I opened the door," said Asha. "I think we scared them off when the taxi came up the driveway. They got away before they could finish the job."

"Was she in the living room like this when you opened the door?"

"She didn't move, and we didn't touch her. We didn't even come inside. I ran for help as soon as I saw what had happened. Who *is* she?"

"Was the front door locked when you came in?"

"I heard the bolt click open when I put my keys in and turned. So, yes, it was locked."

Tanya whirled around, her heart thumping, her eyes darting around the room.

Max was sitting to the side, watching the first responders work on the girl. If the person who did this was still in the house, he'd be barking his head off and racing to catch them.

No. They're far away by now.

"This is all my fault." Tanya rubbed her eyes and pushed away the maddening thoughts that kept telling her Noel was sure to die. "I should have left her in the shelter until we figured this out."

"*What* shelter?" said Asha, impatience laced in her voice.

Katy wobbled toward them. "Who's that girl, Tanya? How did she get inside our house? Who did that to her?"

Tanya pulled her friends by their arms to a corner of the room and lowered her voice.

"She's one of the kids on the murder board. The photo on the end. The girl who looked like a boy."

"Where did you find her?" whispered Asha.

"In the woods, behind Eveline Hart's house."

Asha and Katy exchanged a startled glance.

Tanya looked over Asha's head at the three firefighters who were helping Noel breathe. A stretcher lay by the door and the siren of an ambulance came from the street. She could hear the girl moaning in pain.

Please be okay, she prayed silently.

She turned to Asha. "We need to find out how they got inside. Come with me."

Tanya spun on her heels and stepped toward the basement stairs.

The basement door was open.

Tanya pulled her Glock out and motioned Asha to stay behind her. She crept down the steps and peeked inside the basement suite.

Did Noel let someone in?

She peeked inside.

The room was empty, but Tanya's eyes widened.

The bedside lamp had fallen over. The bedsheets lay crumpled on the floor like Noel had jumped out of bed when the intruder came in. The sandwich plate was upside down on the ground, with crumbs scattered everywhere.

Tanya felt something catch in her throat.

Noel had tried to escape the intruder.

Asha bent down to inspect the crumbs. "She tried to run away."

Tanya nodded. "She opened the basement door and ran upstairs but they followed her."

She stepped inside the suite and walked up to the windows. They were locked down. The curtains were still drawn.

"Door's not locked!"

Tanya turned to see Asha had pushed open the back door.

"Did you forget to lock it?" said Asha.

"I double-checked every exit in the house to make sure she was safe."

"Whoever it was," said Asha, "they came in through here."

Tanya walked over and scrutinized the lock. "They had a key to this house."

"Impossible," came a voice from inside the suite.

Tanya spun around to see Katy shuffling down the basement steps with Max next to her.

"Impossible?" said Tanya. "How so?"

"I have the master keys and you have the spare," said Katy. "My mom only had two sets."

"She could have given another to a neighbor for emergencies," said Asha.

Katy shook her head. "She told me this was a very safe neighborhood."

Tanya raised a brow.

"Call her. Ask her if she made an extra set for anyone else."

Katy nodded and turned around. "Come, Max. Let's go find my handbag."

Asha followed her up the stairs with Tanya behind her, her mind swirling with questions.

The living room had become crowded in their absence.

More first responders had arrived on the scene, but most were just watching the medics work. The fire chief was standing by the doorway, a deep frown on his face.

The paramedics moved Noel onto the stretcher with an oxygen mask on her little face and rushed over to the ambulance. The remaining crew followed them out, talking in low voices.

Tanya stepped up to the chief.

"Someone tried to kill that kid. She needs protection."

"We'll take care of her from now on," said the fire chief with a curt nod. "She'll be in hospital and under medical supervision within minutes."

"I said," said Tanya through clenched teeth, "she needs *protection*."

"Rest assured, ma'am, I'll have my people with her at all times."

"If anything happens to her, I will hold you personally responsible."

The chief gave a start as if he was surprised a civilian would talk to him so aggressively. He glared.

"I believe you have more serious problems to think about right now."

Tanya stared at him.

"What do you mean by that?"

"I hear the sheriff has a few questions for you."

Chapter Twenty-eight

"Stone!"

Tanya's jaw tightened.

Sheriff Reginald was stomping up their driveway. "Do you want to tell me what's going on here?"

Max growled.

Tanya glared. "That's what I'd like to know, too."

The sheriff didn't seem to register her anger or was ignoring it. "Who's that little tramp?"

Tanya's eyes narrowed. "Her name is Noel."

"Who the hell is Noel?"

"She's one of the missing children on Eveline Hart's murder board. I pointed her out to you, Sheriff."

"What was she doing in your house?"

"She and Jodie, that boy who died, were running away from something. I found her malnourished in the back woods and brought her inside to keep her safe."

"Keep her safe, huh? Want to tell me how she ended up almost dead on your living-room floor?"

"That's exactly what I want to know too," said Tanya in a crisp voice.

"You'll have plenty of time to ponder that question." The sheriff pulled out a pair of handcuffs from his belt. "Stone, I'm arresting you for the attempted murder of—"

Tanya stepped up to him, her nose five inches from his. The sheriff gave her a startled look, his handcuffs dangling from his hand.

"If you arrest me now," said Tanya, articulating every syllable through her clenched teeth, "I'm going to haul you to FBI's HQ myself."

A smirk crossed his face.

"You seem to have forgotten our agreement. You'd get into trouble if you did."

"I won't stop you from telling the bureau whatever you want," said Tanya.

She jabbed a finger on his chest.

"I will pay my dues for trespassing Eveline Hart's house. I will pay for any of the misdemeanors I'm guilty of. But if you think you're going to stop me from finding out who stole these kids, did goodness knows what to them, and is now hunting them down, you're wrong."

The sheriff stared at her, his smirk disappearing.

She pulled her phone out. "How would you like my immediate supervisor's number?"

His eyes widened as if he didn't believe her.

"I will share the details with them myself. The FBI will be looking into the death of Jodie, the attempted murder of Noel, and the murder-suicide at Cora's Café."

"Eveline Hart's case isn't related."

"I think differently."

"The feds have no business in my town," growled the sheriff. "Nothing here has crossed state lines. This is a local case."

"Not anymore."

His face turned purple. "That's *my* call."

"That girl who almost got strangled had been missing for years. I found her in the woods, hiding in a shelter that isn't suitable for an animal. I'm sure the bureau will have plenty to say about what was going on here under your watch."

"She's not the only one," came a voice from behind.

Tanya turned.

Asha was walking over, holding her phone up. On the screen was the photo of the murder board, zoomed in on the children's faces.

"There are four more kids. If they're still alive and in the same condition as Tanya found Noel, the FBI will want to know what you've been doing to track them down."

The sheriff glared. A nerve on his neck pulsed. "This is my jurisdiction."

Asha shot him a furious glance. "One of these children was killed, and another was almost killed, all within hours of each other, and you're debating *jurisdiction*?"

"Do you want the blood of these kids on your hands, Sheriff?" said Tanya. "Noel was a foster kid, lost in the system. I'd bet they were all taken from the streets. And I'd bet everything the culprits are hunting them down to stop them from talking." Tanya suppressed the urge to punch the man. "We don't have time to stand here and chitchat."

The sheriff let out an angry hiss. "You don't get to tell me what to do!"

Tanya clicked on her boss's number. Ignoring the officer's icy glare, she left Special Agent in Charge, Paul Desmond a message with details of each crime and a request to send urgent help to find the remaining missing children.

When Tanya hung up, the sheriff's eyes had turned hard as steel. She stepped up to him. "Arrest me. You can explain everything to the feds who'll be here with their own questions for you."

Sheriff Reginald opened his mouth and closed it. Then, without a word, he whirled around and stomped down the driveway, pounding the pavement so hard Tanya was sure the asphalt would crack.

They watched the sheriff get into his vehicle and slam the door shut. Instead of taking off, he pulled out his phone and talked to someone.

Asha shook her head. "A classic megalomaniac."

"He could be behind all this," said Katy from the porch. "I don't trust him one bit."

"Me neither," said Tanya.

Asha turned to her. "We can't hang around until your boss gets a team together. We have to do something."

"Don't worry. I'm not leaving town until we find those kids." Tanya set her lips in a thin grim line. "What happened to Noel is on me. I left her alone when I should have been watching over her."

"You did what you thought was right," said Katy. "Blaming yourself won't help."

Tanya looked up at Katy who was leaning against the banister, her face lined with exhaustion.

"Did you get a hold of your foster mom?"

"Left her a message, but she might be outside cell coverage. I'll try her again soon."

"You're supposed to be resting, Katy," said Asha, her forehead lined with concern.

"Don't worry about me. You guys go look for the kids. The clock is ticking for them. I'll hold the fort here."

Tanya shook her head. "You can't stay here. We need to get you to a safe place."

Katy didn't answer. She was looking over her shoulder at the street, a curious expression on her face. Tanya turned to see Hudson Wyatt walking over with his dog in tow.

Milo bounded over to Max. Max got up, and soon the two dogs were greeting each other. Max stopped his sniffing briefly to growl at Wyatt, then went back to saying hello to the Great Dane.

"Is everything okay, ladies?" said Wyatt.

"We're fine," said Asha, rustling up a polite smile.

"Anything I can do to help at all?"

"We don't need any help," said Tanya, her voice harsher than she intended.

Wyatt looked up at Katy on the porch. "You look a little peaked."

Katy smiled a weak smile. "I feel a lot better now, thanks."

"You're more than welcome to sit by my pool and make yourself comfortable. Read a book and enjoy the ocean view. I also make a darned good lemonade. I hear lemonade is good for an upset stomach."

Can this man get any creepier?

"That won't be happening," snapped Tanya.

Wyatt turned to her.

"I saw the sheriff come over with his handcuffs." A strange glint came over his eyes. "This is not over, you know that, don't you? Looks to me like you might need a good lawyer. I'd be happy to give you a friend's rate."

"I don't require your services."

"I know this town well and most importantly, I know the sheriff."

"Your brother-in-law, you mean?"

Wyatt smiled. "That's exactly why you'll need me on your side."

"Perhaps, that's exactly why I don't need your services."

He shook his head.

"You're way in over your head." The glint came to his eyes again. "You've stirred a hornet's nest. This will not end well."

"I suggest you leave now," she snarled. At her heels, Max growled.

They watched in silence as Hudson Wyatt turned around and strolled down the street toward the sheriff's vehicle. He leaned in to talk to the officer.

Tanya's brow knotted.

She wished she could listen in. Something told her neither man was up to any good.

Chapter Twenty-nine

"Hello?"

The three of them turned.

Their neighbor, Pat, was doddering down her front steps with her cane.

"Girls!"

Asha groaned. "Gosh, is she coming over?"

Katy made a face. "To yell at us vagrants, and tell us to get out of town again."

Pat waved urgently. They watched her in silence, bracing for the insults. She staggered closer.

"Is Noel going to be okay?"

Tanya almost jumped.

She knows the girl's name?

Katy stared at the woman, her mouth open like she couldn't believe her ears.

Pat lumbered over to the fence and leaned against it, like she was exhausted from that short walk.

"I know you girls were trying to save her," she said in a raspy voice. "Thank you." She paused. "Is my girl going to be fine?"

Katy's eyes widened.

"*Your* girl?" spluttered Asha.

"Don't tell her I called her that. She would never allow it after what happened."

"What happened?" said Tanya, frowning.

Pat's mouth turned down, the lines on her forehead making her look older and even more morose than usual.

"I've been looking for her for years. She was my daughter. Kind of, anyway."

"Noel's your *daughter*?" said Katy, finally finding her voice.

"Adopted." Pat glanced down at her shoes, seemingly oblivious to the shock bombs she had been dropping. "She was twelve when my husband got her from a foster home in Seattle."

"Wow," said Katy at this surprising revelation.

"I know." Pat nodded. "Almost an adult. She wasn't the little baby I wanted."

Tanya pulled back. *An adult at twelve?*

Katy opened her mouth, then shut it, as if unsure how to even respond to such a statement.

"Wyatt told us your daughter ran away after your husband died," said Tanya. "Was he referring to Noel?"

"He was."

Pat's voice lowered to a whisper.

"I wanted a little boy all my life. My husband and I tried to have a baby for a long time, but I couldn't, you see."

"I'm sorry to hear that," said Katy, sympathy in her voice.

"The doctors made it clear I would never bear a child. That was when Tom decided to adopt one. He didn't want to hear my thoughts. He forced me to sign the documents."

Asha straightened up. "Your husband can't make you sign anything. That's coercive."

"I come from a different generation than you." Pat gripped the fence tighter. "All I wanted was my own flesh and blood. I wanted a son. Not some strange girl living in my house."

"Do you know why Noel left home?" said Tanya.

Pat sighed heavily.

"She never accepted me as a mother." She paused and looked into the distance. "And I never accepted her as my daughter."

Katy gasped.

"She and Tom got along fine, though. So well, Tom hardly said a word to me, other than to scold me because I was neglecting the kid. He took Noel under his arm. Spent all his time with her. He was very protective about that girl, you see."

Katy and Asha exchanged an alarmed glance.

"He took her to work with him most days," said Pat. "Said it would expand her horizons and educate her better than any school."

Tanya's spidey senses were on full alert.

Does she realize what she's saying?

Pat turned to her, her chin pointed. "I'm not a bad person. I never meant the kid ill. I just didn't want her in my home."

"When did she run away?" said Tanya.

"Three years ago. She knew she was unwanted. She disappeared the day after Tom died."

"How long had Noel been living with you by then?"

"Eight months, or thereabouts." Pat mumbled something under her breath, but Tanya didn't catch it.

"She was what, twelve years old, then?" said Katy.

Pat nodded. Her hand holding the cane was trembling. Sharing family secrets seemed to take a toll on her.

"She just took off to the woods?" said Asha, frowning.

Pat's eyes widened. "Oh, no. She caught a bus back to the children's home in Seattle."

"She got on the bus to the city by herself?" said Katy.

Pat gave a dejected shrug. "I don't know. I locked the front door as soon as she stepped off the porch. I was glad to be rid of her."

Tanya, Asha, and Katy stood in stunned silence. It was a rare occasion when Asha or Katy were stumped for words, and this was one.

"How did your husband die?" said Tanya after a few seconds.

Pat's shoulders drooped.

"Heart attack. Died on the spot."

"My condolences to you," said Katy in a subdued voice.

"Where did this happen?" said Tanya.

"He was driving home from the Manhattan Project lab when he felt his chest constrict. I know because he called me. He was taking a shortcut through the woods. I dialed emergency services but by the time they found his car, he was gone."

Pat's mouth turned down even more.

"I miss him so much. I loved him even after he... I will always love him."

"He loved the girl more than he loved you, didn't he?" said Tanya.

Pat shot her a furious look.

"How dare you!"

She swallowed hard, as if to compose herself.

"You think I'm a bad person, don't you? Yes, I pushed the girl away. I'm not proud of what I did, but I lost my husband, my career, and I could never bear a child. I'm a victim too."

Tanya raised an eyebrow but didn't speak.

She knew most women were aware when their partners abused other family members. They refused to open their eyes because that would mean addressing the ugly, raging bull in the house, and they had little self-esteem to stand up to the bully. So, the horror continued.

"I never saw Noel again until this morning," continued Pat. "That was when I saw her in your backyard. You were trying to hide her, but I recognized her profile."

So, she was watching us.

Pat looked down at her shoes again. "I wanted to talk to her, but I knew she'd never want to see me again."

"Did you know Noel was hurt just now?" said Katy.

Pat wiped her eyes. "Blake told me."

"Do you have any idea who would try to hurt her?" said Asha.

"If I knew, I would tell you." She paused. "I was making tea in the kitchen."

"Do you have a spare key to our house, by any chance?" said Tanya, eyeing her.

Pat blinked and turned to Katy.

"Your foster mother didn't like me. She thought I was a mean woman who didn't deserve children."

Katy put a hand on her arm. "I'm sure she would never say anything so horrible."

Pat shook her head. "Don't be so polite. Just tell the truth. That's what I do. It's better that way."

Tanya wondered what a sad life this woman had had.

When Pat spoke again, her voice was firm, like she had gathered strength. She turned to Katy.

"I heard you needed a place to stay while your friends searched for the lost kids."

Tanya narrowed her eyes. Everyone seemed to have ears the size of elephants in this town.

"How did you know?"

"If I stand in the hallway next to that small window." Pat pointed to the side of her home. "I can hear everything going on in this driveway."

"What do you know about the other boys?"

Pat looked up at Tanya. "Only what I heard you tell the sheriff just now. You said there were four more boys, and you needed to find them, right?"

No one replied.

Pat wiped something from her eye.

"It's too late for me to make amends for Noel. I feel terrible, especially after Blake told me what happened to her. The least I can do is do my bit to help you find the remaining children."

She gave her a pleading look.

"I know you don't believe me. I will pay for being a terrible person one day."

Before Tanya could say anything, Katy leaned across the fence and squeezed Pat's arm.

"You're doing the right thing," she said. "Actually, I'm a bit tired and would love a quiet place to sit with a cup of tea for an hour or two. Can I come in?"

Chapter Thirty

"Pat's husband died on this road," said Asha.

She and Tanya had been bumping along the unpaved hiking trails in the woods for the past half an hour. Asha had her phone open to her GPS, and was scouring for signs of human-made structures nearby.

"The closest Manhattan Project site is miles away in Hanford," she said. "That's nowhere near the coast."

"Tom was lying to Pat," said Tanya. "I doubt there's a special research lab anywhere here. We're looking for a large cabin or a barn, a place where they can keep the kids away from the prying eyes of the town."

The road they were on seemed to have potholes the size of moon craters. Tanya's Jeep was designed for off-roading, but one bad turn in this terrain would mean getting stuck in the middle of nowhere.

Tanya kept her eyes in front and both hands on the wheel, but something else was bothering her even more.

Katy had refused to go to a public place like the hospital, saying she felt safer with the neighbor. She was sure she could stand up to a woman who could barely take a few steps without a cane.

Plus, she had Max by her side.

Tanya and Asha left her in Pat's home, with Asha's bear spray can in her pocket, and strict instructions to lock herself in the guest bedroom if she saw or heard anything strange. And to not eat or drink anything anyone offered.

Even Pat.

Tanya needed Max on this search mission, but she felt a hundred times better knowing Katy wasn't alone.

"You never told me who you thought the two men on the murder board were," said Tanya.

"It's a wild guess, but one of them is Tom, Pat's husband, and the other is Eveline Hart's husband."

"Both died from sudden heart attacks before they hit fifty."

Asha nodded. "I could be wrong, but I think someone found out what they had been doing and killed them."

"That's what I suspect too, but we'll need to dig up evidence. If they were murdered, the trail will be cold."

"If they were heading a pedophile ring in this town, I really don't care how they died."

Tanya's heart agreed with her friend, but her trained FBI head told her otherwise.

A murder is still a murder.

"I felt sick when Pat said Tom took a twelve-year-old kid to work regularly."

Tanya nodded. "Noel was showing classic signs of abuse. She looked traumatized when I found her. Jodie, too."

"Pat had to know what was going on," said Asha. "She was jealous of Tom's attention to Noel, and blamed the girl. It's not the first time we've seen this kind of family dysfunction."

"Pat could have been clueless but Eveline Hart found out for sure," said Tanya. "Her boys were tangled up in this too. Eric had that heart branding on his skin, just like Jodie and Noel."

"But why would Eveline kill her own son?" said Asha.

Tanya's eyes narrowed as she spotted a large branch across the trail. She slowed down to roll over it. Asha grabbed the door handle as the Jeep's tires bounced up and down.

"My guess is he was involved too," said Tanya as she straightened the vehicle. "He could have been a victim turned captor."

Asha turned to her. "I don't like leaving Noel with the fire chief. How do we know he's not part of this, too?"

"There was nothing we could have done about that," said Tanya "If I'd stopped them from taking her, they would have restrained me, and I can't help her from jail."

"A pedophile ring in a small town like this could only mean one thing," said Asha. "There are lots more people involved. Maybe the fire chief. Maybe even the sheriff."

"Sheriff Reginald's primary motive is to maintain his status as the big cheese of this town." Tanya spoke slowly, as if she was thinking it through. "He could also be seeking power in other, illegal ways."

"What if he's clean?" said Asha.

"He'd rally his team and start a proper search to beat the feds. He'd want to come out looking good. But people are unpredictable and you never know how they will react. Especially someone with psychopathic tendencies."

"And if he's corrupt?"

Tanya paused for a second.

"We have to be prepared for war."

Asha's phone buzzed.

It was Katy. She read the message out loud for Tanya.

Found photos in Pat's bedroom.

Asha typed back.

And??

Katy replied.

2nd man on murder board is Pat's hubby. Think Tom was abusing kids.

Tanya nodded. "We already came to that conclusion." She paused. "What's Katy doing?"

"Investigating."

A buzz made Asha turn back to her phone.

"She found something in the pile. I presume she means the pile of photos."

Before Asha could type her question, another buzz came. Asha read the message out loud.

"Fifteen miles from Sunset Drive. North. There's something at the edge of woods."

Tanya straightened in her seat and checked the compass on her dash. They were heading in the right direction.

"Route co-ordinates?"

"On it." Asha typed furiously.

Tanya kept driving, keeping her eyes peeled, while her friends figured things out.

"Found it!"

Asha was zooming on her GPS map. "There's a rectangle structure fourteen miles ahead. It's the only thing around here, and it's where Katy said it should be."

"What are we looking at?"

"Hard to say. She found a map of the woods with the photos. Someone, presumably Tom, had drawn a large rectangle on it with a pencil. She also found a photo of what looks like a warehouse in the woods."

"So, this is a wild guess."

"Better than nothing."

"Where's Pat? Is she helping Katy find all this?"

"She's sleeping in the living room and has no idea."

"So, Katy's snooping?"

"Rummaging through Pat's house. Why do you think she fought to stay? She wants to feel useful. I don't blame her, and we can't stop her now."

"You two will be the death of me, I swear," said Tanya as she pushed on the gas. "What's the terrain by the warehouse like?"

Asha glanced at her screen. "Slightly elevated, but I don't see cliffs, rivers, or major hazards. Just dense wood."

"Can we sneak around the back?"

"If we stick to the tree line, but we don't know what security is like. They could have electrified fences, barbed wire, concrete blocks, armed guards. Even dogs."

"We'll cross that bridge when we get to it."

When they got to half a mile of their destination, Tanya stopped and put the Jeep in reverse. "Hold on tight," she said, as she did a three-way turn and swiveled the vehicle sideways.

"What are you doing?" said Asha, glancing around her. "We still have a bit more to go."

"We're jumping the ditch first."

Tanya maneuvered over to the edge of the road, changed the gear into four-wheel-drive-low, and took manual control of her vehicle. She pressed on the gas and rolled into the narrow gully. The Jeep swayed. Asha clutched the dashboard.

Tanya navigated the vehicle across the ditch and pulled into the woods. She winced as twigs and thorns scraped against the panels and tree branches drummed the sides of the Jeep. She kept rolling.

I can always get the dents fixed, but I have only one chance to find those kids alive.

She drove behind a clump of shrubs, put the car in park, and pulled her Glock out. She inserted a magazine and racked the slide.

"I wish I had mine," said Asha, pulling out the knife she had plucked from their kitchen before leaving. "This won't be much of a help against who knows what they have."

"You'll be my eyes and ears," said Tanya. "Stay alert, watch for shadows, and stick behind me."

Tanya jumped out of the Jeep and closed the door. Asha clicked on her GPS and led the way.

It took them twenty minutes to cross the thicket and hike toward the rectangular gray block on Asha's map. They didn't see it until they were twenty yards from it.

A murder of black crows rose in alarm from the dense brushwood as they approached, cawing like they were warning them to stay away.

Asha gasped as she spotted the crumbling structure between the trees.

"That's no warehouse. It's like the set of a horror movie."

Tanya stared at the concrete bunker.

"More like an abandoned Second World War prison camp."

Chapter Thirty-one

Tanya and Asha remained concealed behind the trees.

Asha shuddered. "You could scream your lungs out here, and no one would hear."

Tanya's stomach turned. "No better place to carry out cruel crimes."

One half of the building was crumbling, with rusted steel bars and broken concrete pillars exposed to the elements. But it was the west half that interested Tanya the most. The intact portion of the structure even had a steel staircase that spiraled up to the second floor.

While it was tempting to climb it, Tanya knew they would be sitting ducks. There had to be another way in.

Think, girl, think.

All the doors, except one, had been barricaded, and all the windows had been boarded. At first glance, it looked abandoned, but a low hum from nearby told Tanya an electric generator was providing power to the building.

She pulled out her phone while Asha snapped photographs.

She typed in the coordinates of their location and sent a note with their latest discovery to Desmond. He still hadn't checked his messages, and that was troubling.

"This is where a mad scientist would work," Asha was saying. "Maybe this was part of the Manhattan Project, after all."

"You think they studied atomic bomb technologies here?"

"It's the perfect location. Close to the shore front to get supplies from ships and concealed in the woods so no one would notice. Plus, there's a cute little town nearby where the workers could live."

"Paradise Cove," said Tanya with a grimace.

Asha surveyed the building. "You know what's weird? There's no graffiti anywhere."

"I guess even the local kids don't dare to come here," said Tanya.

"Maybe they know something bad is going on."

"It's a miracle Jodie and Noel escaped this place."

"Resourceful kids," said Asha, "and brave as heck. It must have taken a lot of guts to find a way out."

Tanya turned to her friend. "These people already poisoned Jodie and tried to kill Noel. We have to be prepared to find the other boys—"

"Don't say it." Asha's face tightened. "We're going to find them alive."

Tanya's brow furrowed. "The problem is we don't know who's in charge or how many people are inside."

She scanned the concrete bunker again.

There was no sign of life, but she could sense people nearby.

A large steel door stood in the far corner of the structure. It was the only entrance that hadn't been barricaded, but without a backup team, Tanya knew barging in would be a foolish proposition.

Something glinted from the side of the building. She whirled around, her heart skipping a beat.

"What is it?" whispered Asha.

Tanya squinted in between the tree branches. "A vehicle. Parked on the east side."

They stared in its direction, trying to make out the car, but all they could see was an occasional glint of something metallic.

The steel door scraped open, making them freeze.

A lone male stepped out, carrying what looked like an automatic rifle.

Asha gasped. "It's the dead man. Eric Hart." She turned to her phone and scrolled to the photos they had found in Eveline Hart's kitchen. "But that's impossible."

Tanya shook her head. "It has to be Eric's brother, Sam. They look similar."

Sam Hart glanced around, his back bowed, his hands clutching his weapon like he was prepared for an ambush. He treaded along the wall, swiveling his head from side to side.

"I know an M16 when I see one," whispered Tanya. "That's some serious and expensive firepower."

Soon, Sam Hart disappeared around the building.

Tanya's heart beat faster.

"This is where they keep the kids." She stepped back and slinked into the woods. "This way. Stay behind me."

Asha followed Tanya as she threaded quietly, keeping to the shadows, but always with the building in their line of sight. They stopped every few minutes to take photos and scour for discreet entrances.

"A heavy-duty pickup truck," said Asha, as the vehicle that had glinted at them came into view. "Looks like the one his brother crashed into the café."

They weaved in between the trees, stepping alongside the north side of the building. They were halfway down when Tanya halted and put a hand out to stop Asha.

Tanya pushed the tree branches aside to get a better look in front of them.

"What is it?" whispered Asha, peering in the direction Tanya was looking.

On the ground, ten yards from where they stood was an elevated flat surface, covered by weeds and moss. Tanya stepped around the pine trees and entered the small clearing.

"The terrain is uneven with tree roots all over the place." She kneeled down in the center. "But this spot is a perfect rectangle. This can't be natural."

Asha brushed the dead leaves aside with her boot and stepped on it with both feet. A metallic clang made her jump.

Tanya's heart beat faster. "There's something under here."

Using their boots and branches they swept the moss and leaves away. Underneath the debris was a large metal lid with a round handle.

"Looks like an ancient drain cover," said Asha.

Tanya pulled on the handle.

It didn't budge.

"Why would anyone put a manhole in the middle of the woods?" Asha stopped as she realized what they had stumbled across. "This is a hatch!"

"This hasn't been opened in decades," said Tanya. "Probably built during the war, in case the enemy attacked. I'd bet there's a fortified bomb shelter underneath the bunker and this is the exit."

Asha's eyes were shining.

"If this provides an escape route out of the building, it will also allow us into the building."

"Exactly."

Chapter Thirty-two

O ther than the low hum of the electric generator, the woods were silent.

Tanya bent down to examine the hatch. An ancient and rusty padlock held the latch down.

"Funny they would lock this from the outside," said Asha.

"This is ancient," said Tanya. "The authorities probably sealed everything up when they shut this place down after the war. They didn't expect a gang to take over their ruined building decades later."

She pulled out her phone. "I need to tell the boss."

Asha looked at her own cell and clicked on the message app. "Didn't expect to get cellular coverage here."

"They should have a signal booster near the bunker. These people have a good setup here." Tanya turned to Asha. "Can you check up on Katy and Max?"

Asha was already typing.

"Is your boss coming over with a SWAT team soon?"

"I don't think he even picked up my messages yet."

"Pat's still sleeping in her chair in the living room," said Asha after messaging their friend. "Katy and Max are in the kitchen, waiting for us."

"Tell her to try her foster mom again. If we find out who has a spare key, we'll find the unsub who tried to kill Noel."

"Katy promised to let us know as soon as she finds out," said Asha, slipping her phone in her pocket. She turned to Tanya. "Are we expecting a truckload of FBI agents to swoop in?"

Tanya stared at the hatch.

"Rustling up an attack team and getting the logistics set up will take hours, maybe even days. The longer we wait, the greater the risk we find those kids dead."

She pocketed her phone, got on her knees, and pulled at the padlock.

It held.

She plucked out the tweezers from her Swiss army knife and stuck it into the lock. Then, she pulled out the toothpick from the knife's toolkit, pushed it inside the lock, and jiggled the pins.

Asha remained behind her, watching the perimeter, as Tanya worked furiously.

The rust wasn't helping. Tanya wanted to bang it with a rock or even shoot it open, but that could alert Sam and whoever else was inside the bunker.

Normally, it would have taken her less than sixty seconds to break this lock, but by the time she heard the click of the lock spring open, she was sweating like a fiend.

Relief rushed through her.

She twisted the padlock off and pulled the rusty steel latch back. The cover squeaked in protest as she tugged on the handle, but it opened.

Her heart raced.

She pulled the hatch all the way back and rested it on its side, surprised it hadn't got stuck. She peeked into the gaping hole, but it was pitch black.

Tanya turned on her phone's flashlight and leaned into the void. A strong musty smell greeted her nose. The narrow pit seemed to disappear into the bowels of the earth.

"A rung ladder," she whispered as she peeked inside.

Asha kneeled down to look into the mouth of the hole. "Do I go first or you?"

Tanya shook her head. "I'm armed. You're not. Close the hatch after me, and stay in the woods for backup."

Asha snapped her head up. "I'm not staying here to be a target if Sam Hart comes prowling. It will be my kitchen knife against his M16."

Tanya didn't have time to argue, not in the open. She stepped onto the iron ladder, putting her weight on the first rung while holding on to the top of the pit. To her relief, it didn't crumble into pieces like she had imagined.

She took another step down gingerly.

Every second they stayed on top meant they risked getting discovered, but she couldn't brazenly jump into this unknown cavern either.

"First things first. I'm going to see if I can open this from the inside."

"Copy that," said Asha.

Swallowing the claustrophobia rising inside of her, Tanya climbed down until only her head was visible from the top. The tunnel was so narrow, her shoulders scraped the sides. She closed the lid over her, waited for a few seconds, and tried to open it again. It took all her strength to push the metal hatch open, but it pushed back.

"It works," came Asha's voice from above her.

Leaving Asha to manage the lid, Tanya inched down, feeling each rung, using her flashlight to guide the way.

She had descended several feet when she heard Asha step into the hole and lower the hatch over her head. A loud crash echoed through the underground space as the cover fell back into position.

Tanya cringed.

She kept climbing down into the void.

It took another twenty feet for her to hit the bottom. She stepped off the last rung and into a small cave. There was an opening on the other end that led to a crudely carved tunnel that seemed to have been burrowed a century earlier.

She touched the sunflower pendant on her neck. She wasn't superstitious, but there were times she wished for her dead mother's protection. This was one.

Asha scrambled down fast, safe in the knowledge her friend had already tested the rungs. She jumped the last few feet, with a sheepish look on her face.

"I'm hoping no one heard that," she whispered, pointing at the hatch on top.

Tanya shrugged. *What's done is done.* "If they're waiting for us, they had better be prepared for a fight."

She turned and shone the flashlight into the tunnel.

"It's warm in here," whispered Asha, opening her jacket zipper.

"The air isn't fresh," said Tanya, searching the walls for vents. "That's not good. We could suffocate."

"Good to know," said Asha, pulling out her phone and fiddling with an app.

"What are you doing?"

"Turning video recording on. If we die down here, they'll at least hear our last words."

With an impatient shake of her head, Tanya stepped into the tunnel. She wondered if anyone had been down here since the Second World War.

The air got warmer the farther they walked, and a strange putrid smell clung to them.

"What's that stink?" Asha put her hand over her nose. "It's like a family of raccoons fell inside and died down here."

"Raccoons are smart, but not smart enough to break a lock. I doubt anything came down that hatch for years."

They had walked about forty yards when the tunnel expanded into what looked like an underground cave. A massive steel door stood at the other end.

Behind her, Asha gagged. "It stinks worse in here."

"I think we're coming to the end," whispered Tanya, stepping over to the door.

Asha clutched her arm. "Oh, my gosh!"

Tanya whirled around. "What?"

"This is why this place smells," said Asha, pointing.

That was when Tanya noticed the human remains in the corner.

Chapter Thirty-three

It was a small body.

It lay in a fetal position, and sufficiently decomposed to show the partial skull and spine.

Tanya stepped closer and focused her light on it.

"Oh, my gosh," said Asha, her hand over her mouth, trying not to retch. "It had to be a kid or a small woman."

Tanya turned her light around the cave.

"There's another one," she said, her voice grim.

Asha turned to her in alarm. "Maybe they came down the hatch and got stuck?"

Tanya stared at the remains of the two small humans, her stomach churning.

"The hatch looked like it hadn't been touched for years, but look at these bodies. They're not fully decomposed yet. Someone left these kids here to die recently, or they were put in here after death."

Asha looked around her, eyes wide in horror. "What *is* this place?"

"A good place to discard the remains of murder victims."

Asha pointed at the thick steel door. "Can we get out of here? I'm going to throw up."

Tanya stepped up to scrutinize the door. It looked like what you would see on a bank vault, one with a round steel handle in the middle.

She placed her ear on the door to listen, but either it was soundproofed or there was no one on the other side.

"This is new," whispered Asha. "I don't think it's an original from the Second World War period."

Tanya didn't answer, but crossed her fingers. If they couldn't get this door open, the only way inside the building would be from the surface, where they would be exposed.

Please work.

She turned the steel handle. It resisted at first, but with Asha's help, they turned it one hundred and eighty degrees till it locked into position.

"Ready?" Tanya whispered.

They heaved.

The heavy, thick door opened a few inches. A peek inside showed another anteroom. A naked fluorescent light bulb illuminated the empty space.

They pulled the door a few more inches, so the gap was large enough for them to squeeze through. They slipped into the anteroom.

"Fresher here," said Asha, taking a deep breath.

"Air vents," said Tanya, turning her flashlight off.

The lone light flickered over their heads, like it was warning them. It was eerily silent in this underground chamber, but Tanya couldn't shake the feeling of people close by.

About five yards ahead, at the other end of the room was what looked like a large opening. A faint blue light gleamed from that direction.

With her Glock aimed forward, she crept toward the opening. She halted.

Asha bumped into her and gasped.

They were looking out into an open hall with high ceilings. It had no windows and just one closed door.

It was cool in here, like air was being pumped from somewhere. The tunnel had been on a slight elevation, but Tanya was sure they were still underground.

A long steel table sat along one wall of this room.

On it was a row of laptops. An array of high-end cameras had been secured to steel stands and attached to the table. Small electronic apparatus that looked like remotes and flash drives lay on the bench.

Expensive equipment, thought Tanya.

On the other end of the wall was a mattress, surrounded by soft box and ring lights, some under umbrella kits. There were crumpled sheets on the mattress, like someone had been sleeping and had just got up. One of the box lights had been turned on, giving the only light to this large space.

Tanya scoured the corners of the hall, looking for hidden shadows. Except for the fancy tech lineup on the table, it was a spartan space.

And empty.

But Tanya and Asha had seen this setup before, in previous investigations. It didn't take a genius to figure out what this room was used for. If there had been any doubt what the children had been subjected to, Tanya was sure now.

Noel's frail and innocent face sprang to her mind, and a flash of fiery anger spiraled up her spine. It was time to find the people who tortured these kids.

There was one exit from this room and it was at the far corner. That door was closed. She squinted around the hall.

"What's that covering the walls?"

"Sound absorber foam," said Asha. "No one can hear what happens down here."

A shiver went down Tanya's spine.

"Check for security cameras," she whispered, as she scanned the ceiling and the walls.

"We need to get the laptops," whispered Asha urgently. "We take those to the FBI and nail the bastards."

Tanya nodded.

After another scan to make sure they wouldn't trip any alarms, Tanya stepped out of the tunnel with Asha at her heels. They were only five feet from the computer table when the door scraped open.

They dove under the table. It wouldn't take much for anyone coming in to spot them, but they still had an element of surprise to their advantage.

Tanya hid under the bench and aimed her Glock at the door.

Chapter Thirty-four

The door opened halfway.

A teen boy shuffled inside.

He was in T-shirt and shorts. He didn't appear as gaunt as Noel had been, or as scruffy as Jodie, but his thin body, hunched back, and pale face told her they had broken his spirit a long time ago.

He plodded across the room, his head hung low. He stepped over to the mattress, his gait laborious, like he was walking to his execution. He didn't flinch when the steel door shut with a clang behind him.

It was like he had come into this room a thousand times and knew exactly what would transpire next. Through the dim light, Tanya caught sight of the branded heart on the back of his left hand.

Her heart beat faster. She kept her sidearm aimed at the door, ready for the adult to walk in.

What are you waiting for?

But the door remained closed.

The kid squatted on the mattress and dropped his head into his hands.

Tanya and Asha stared at him, knowing they should go toward him, but unsure how he would react to their sudden presence.

A low buzz made Tanya jump.

It was Asha's phone. She spun around and put a finger on her lips, but the boy hadn't heard, absorbed in his misery.

Asha pulled her phone out. It was Katy. She turned the screen toward Tanya.

The message read, *Got hold of foster mom.*

Asha typed back.

And???

Katy answered.

She gave spare keys to Pat.

Asha and Tanya exchanged an alarming glance. A second buzz made Asha jump, she almost hit her head on top of the table.

Found rat poison under sink + muffin tray in dishwasher.

Asha's eyes widened. She typed.

Get out!

Katy replied.

Pat's still sleeping. Good time to investigate.

Tanya grabbed the phone and typed.

OUT! NOW!

Katy's answer came, slower this time.

OK. OK.

Tanya typed again.

Go to woods. Don't talk to anyone. Stay with Max till I give OK.

They waited for Katy to reply, but this time, they didn't hear back. After a few seconds, Asha turned to Tanya, her eyes filled with anxiety.

"We have to get back," she whispered.

Tanya scrunched her forehead. Something didn't add up.

It was their conversation with Pat that gave them the clues to where the kids were kept. If she was part of this gang, why would she have shared information that would lead them to the lion's den?

How did the rat poison and muffin tray get in her kitchen? Was someone trying to frame Pat?

Tanya glanced at the boy on the mattress. He had buried his head in his hands. The slight up and down motion of his chest told her he was crying silently.

She scanned the room, but no one had come in while they had been texting with Katy.

"Keep watch," she whispered.

She scooted out from under the table. She stepped toward the boy, her weapon behind her, but at the ready in case anyone barged in. The kid was so distraught, he didn't see her until she was three feet from him.

He jumped back with a cry and scrambled to the end of the mattress. He stared at her like she was a phantom. His eyes were so glazed, Tanya wondered if they had been feeding him drugs to make him compliant.

"Don't be scared," she said.

The boy jerked up at the sound of her voice, then scurried back on his haunches until he hit the wall. Realizing he was cornered, he wrapped his arms around himself and stared at her, shaking in fright.

Tanya crouched down a few feet from him.

Like Noel and Jodie, she was sure he was a few years older than he looked. Traffickers broke down their victims physically, emotionally, and mentally soon after capture. That crushed their spirit, stunted their growth, and kept them subdued.

"Hey," whispered Tanya. "I came to get you away from here."

The boy stared at her like he didn't understand. She offered a hand to him. He shrank back.

"Don't hurt me."

Tanya's heart sank. Those were the same words Noel had said to her from inside her shelter. Now she knew what she had been hiding from.

"It's okay," she said. "I'm going to take you away from these people who hurt you."

That was when the door banged open.

Tanya leaped to her feet, her Glock at the ready.

Blake?

Deputy Blake stepped in, and without a word, raised his hand. His black gun glistened in the pale light.

Tanya heard a gasp from Asha under the table. She prayed she wouldn't jump out to defend her. All Asha had on her was a kitchen knife.

"Hey, you! Stop right there!" shouted Blake, his voice echoing through the hall.

Tanya didn't move. Her aim didn't waver either.

Her head spun. The past few hours had felt like being on a roller coaster without the seat belt on. She was holding on but getting whiplash at every turn.

"You crazy, interfering bitch," Blake spat out. "He told me to keep an eye on you."

Tanya's ears pricked up.

"Who runs this sick business, Blake?" she called out. "Sheriff Reginald? Someone else?"

Blake glared.

Tanya's brain whirred. Blake was Pat's nephew and did daily wellness checks at her home. He had visited Pat's house the day

Katy got poisoned. He had also been first on the scene when Jodie was found dead in Pat's backyard.

"Drop your weapon," snarled Tanya.

"I'll shoot you first," growled Blake.

"Your game's up!" came a third voice. "The building's surrounded."

Blake jerked back, startled to hear the disembodied voice.

It was Asha from under the table, projecting her voice so loudly it echoed from all the corners of the hall, spooking even Tanya.

"You're done, Blake. Give yourself up."

Tanya didn't dare glance at her friend, and prayed she wouldn't do anything rash.

"Who... who are you...?" Blake swung around, searching the dark corners of the room. "Who else is in here?"

Asha laughed from the shadows. "It's the ghost of your criminal past."

Tanya winced, wishing her friend would stop playing this dangerous game. She knew Asha was only trying to unsettle him, but Blake's weapon was pointed directly at her chest.

Blake swiveled his head. "Who are you?" His voice raised in pitch. "Where are you? Show yourself!"

"You're a dead man," cackled Asha.

He was getting nervous, and nervous people make unpredictable moves.

The kid was crouched by her feet, watching all this go down. If Blake became unhinged, there would be a bloodbath in here.

Chapter Thirty-five

"Place your sidearm on the floor," said Tanya, keeping her voice level.

"Go ahead and shoot me," said Blake, "I'll kill you and that kid before I die."

Get the boy out of the line of fire.

Tanya took a discreet step away from the child.

"You're a pervert in uniform," came Asha's voice. "The worst type of criminal."

"I never touched them!" yelled Blake.

"Right," said Tanya. "Tell that to the jury."

"I'm just here for security. I have nothing to do with their streaming pedo site."

Tanya raised an eyebrow. "That didn't bother you?"

He glared.

Tanya's brain raced, as she put the puzzle pieces together. Blake was a goon, but she was sure he did more than just protect this property.

"You'll be going to prison for the rest of your life."

She stepped closer to him. Her gun was aimed right between his eyes, just like his weapon was pointing at her face.

"I'm sure you'll have a wonderful time," laughed Asha.

"Come out!" Blake shouted, panic rising in his voice. "Come out, you coward!"

Tanya could see the anonymous voice unnerved him. For all he knew, the hand belonging to it could have a weapon pointing at him.

"How do we end this?" said Tanya, taking another small step closer. "Your aunt Pat told us all about you."

It was a lie, but a needed one.

His eyes bulged. *"Aunt Pat told you?"*

"You took our house keys from her home, didn't you?"

Blake shot her a wild look.

"It was you who delivered the poisoned muffins. You left a plate on her porch too, but I bet hers were fine. You poisoned Jodie with an opioid overdose and you tried to strangle Noel."

Tanya kept her aim steady.

"That's why you were so keen to get me out of the house. Thankfully Noel is stronger than you thought."

Blake's hand holding the gun was now shaking.

Asha guffawed from her hideout. "We know everything."

Tanya took another step forward.

She was close enough to lunge at him. Asha's games had given her an advantage. His attention was diffused and his face registered confusion.

"You weren't struggling with smoke inhalation when I came to pull you out of Eveline's house," said Tanya. "You set the fire."

Blake glowered.

"When you saw me drive by, you played the victim so I wouldn't suspect you. You're a dirty cop but a darned good actor."

183

"You can't prove any of that!" shouted Blake, sweat pouring down his face.

Bingo.

"The FBI doesn't miss a thing," said Tanya. "Do you think we wouldn't see what you did?"

That wasn't true, but it had the impact she had been hoping for.

Blake's jaw dropped. "FBI? You're FBI?"

His face flushed and his eyes darkened.

"You bitch—"

Tanya leaped on him, pinning his arms back.

His legs buckled under her weight and he fell to the floor with a crash. Their guns flew into opposite corners of the room. They rolled on the ground, kicking, punching, grunting.

Tanya grabbed his right arm and twisted it. Blake roared in pain.

She saw his fist rise. The blow to her face almost blinded her. He pulled her by the collar and slammed her head on the hard concrete floor.

"Stop or I'll shoot!"

Tanya and Blake froze in mid fight.

Asha had scrambled out from under the table and grabbed the two sidearms. For all the games she had played, her hands were shaking. But the weapons were now pointing at both of them.

"I said, stop!" shouted Asha.

Tanya knew what she needed to do. Get away from Blake, so Asha could get a clean shot.

She pulled away, but Blake yanked her back, his hands wrapping around her neck. Tanya rammed her fingers into the soft spot by his Adam's apple. His hands slipped off her throat.

She jumped to her feet and spun around. Before he knew what was happening, she jumped on his right knee.

Blake howled in pain.

Once more.

She kicked hard, this time on his kneecap. The sickening scrunch of his bone breaking echoed through the hall. He clutched his leg and wailed.

Tanya stepped away and wiped the sweat off her face. She bent over and placed her hands on her thighs to catch her breath. Adrenaline was still pumping through her veins and her heart was racing a million miles a second. She wondered if Blake would ever walk again.

"I was trying to distract him," said Asha, the guns limp in her hands.

"They know we're here now," said Tanya, panting.

Asha pointed at the walls. "This room is soundproofed. I don't think anyone heard anything."

"We need to find the other kids and get them out ASAP. We can't take any more risks."

Tanya turned to the boy huddled by the mattress.

"Where are the other kids?"

"Please don't hurt me," he whimpered.

"We came to save you," said Tanya, her voice sharper than she had intended. "Tell us where the others are. We don't have time."

The boy scrunched further into a ball and covered his face.

"I can't walk!" screeched Blake from the floor. "Get EMT! Do something!"

Karma is a bitter pill to swallow, thought Tanya with a grimace. She didn't even look his way.

"Here," said Asha, nudging Tanya aside. "Let me do this."

She handed Tanya her Glock and squatted by the boy. There was an advantage to being petite. Asha was almost as tall as the teen and much less intimidating than Tanya was.

"What's your name, hun?" said Asha.

The boy gave her a frightened look. "L... Liam."

"Liam, we're going to take you home, okay?"

The boy started trembling.

Behind them, Blake yelled something incomprehensible, but no one was paying attention to him anymore.

Asha put her arm around the kid's shoulders. "No one's going to hurt you again, hun."

He looked at her like he wasn't sure he could believe her.

"I promise you that," said Asha.

"C... can my f... friends come too?" His voice was squeaky, but there was hope in his eyes.

"We're not going to leave anybody behind. Where are your friends right now, hun?"

"In our room." He wiped his tears from the back of his hand. "He locks us inside."

"Who locks you in?" said Tanya.

"S... Sam," stammered the boy.

"Help me!" shrieked Blake. "I'm going to die!"

Tanya's mind whirred as she considered the logistics of finding the other boys and getting them out safely.

"How many adults are in this building?" she asked.

Liam shrugged. "I dunno."

"Where's the room your friends are in?"

"Second floor," whispered Liam, without looking up. "At the corner of the hall."

With a nod to Asha, Tanya marched across the room, stepping around Blake who was now curled into a fetal position, tears of pain running down his face.

She threaded over to the door, her Glock aimed forward.

It's time to find out who runs this sick show.

Tanya reached for the door handle and pushed it down. She had opened the door halfway when a gunshot rang out.

An anguished scream echoed through the building.

Chapter Thirty-six

T anya froze in place.

The gunshot and scream had come from above.

It was strange how quickly an eerie silence settled in the air soon after.

There were no further shots, cries, shouts, or even the sound of someone running. It was like a magician had waved a wand and frozen everything.

Tanya stared through the narrow gap of the doorway.

She was looking into a green room, one you would expect to find next to a recording studio or an auditorium where participants waited for their turn to take the stage.

It was small and windowless with a large coffee station in one corner. Comfortable leather couches and glass coffee tables had been arranged on a rich rug. Stacks of brochures and journals sat on the tables. Tanya couldn't make the words out, but grimaced to think what kind of magazines they might be.

This was the room where the adults convened, before walking into the underground chamber to commit horrific acts to children in front of video cameras.

All in the name of entertaining the dark web.

There better be a special place in hell for these monsters.

Behind Tanya, she could hear Liam's panicked breathing. She turned around and made eye contact with Asha.

"Get out of here, now," she whispered.

Asha balked. "I'm not leaving without you," she whispered hoarsely.

Tanya's eyes fell on the boy. He was shaking and clutching her friend's arm, desperately trying to hide behind her.

"You need to take him to safety. I'll bring the others."

Tanya stood by the doorway, while Asha pulled the boy to his feet gently. Asha turned around and ushered him into the tunnel.

On the floor, Blake had turned strangely quiet. He was still hugging his knee and wincing in pain, but the gunshot seem to have silenced him. She knew better than to demand what was going on. He would only waste her time, and the other kids were still up there.

Alone and in danger.

Tanya waited for Asha and Liam to disappear into the tunnel before stepping out. Her eyes and ears were alert and her sidearm was ready.

Glad her boot soles were made of soft rubber, she treaded across the green room and opened the door at the end. A concrete stairway greeted her eyes.

She stood by the threshold.

Hearing nothing, she tiptoed up the steps, halting every few feet to listen. When she got closer to the top, she stopped and craned her neck.

Her jaw dropped as she took stock of the first floor.

Despite the crumbling old-war façade, the interior of this bunker had been modernized.

Dark wood paneling covered the boarded-up windows. Bookshelves lined the walls, and small groups of leather sofas and coffee tables were placed around the room. Persian rugs carpeted the floor, and a chandelier hung from the high ceiling above. The dozen green bankers' lamps on the coffee tables gave the space a warm glow.

A well-stocked, long bar was set against one wall. The dark wooden counter gleamed under the chandelier lighting.

This room looked more like a wealthy family's luxurious library, rather than the inside of a dilapidated bunker in the middle of nowhere. It was an exclusive lounge reserved for those with expensive taste.

There were only two exits to this large open space.

One was the main steel door in front of the building which Sam Hart had used earlier. The other was a much narrower wooden door to the side, which Tanya hadn't noticed before.

An oppressive silence seemed to hang in the air, but there was no sign of Sam Hart. Or his massive gun.

For a moment, Tanya wondered if the gunshot and that scream had been a figment of her imagination.

Her eyes surveyed the space but she couldn't see any cameras or overt surveillance equipment. Either they were hidden among the panels or none had been installed to ensure the privacy of their clients.

She turned around, taking it all in, feeling sick to her stomach.

Whoever ran this show had sunk a good amount of money to refurbish this place.

From her bureau training, she knew child sexual exploitation was a lucrative business. Human trafficking was an overall 150-billion-dollar global industry with a worldwide network of pedophile video and photo sites that brought in solid profits.

For one second, Tanya wanted to stomp back down and put a bullet through Blake's head. Even if he had only been a henchman for this gang, he didn't deserve to live after supporting such a heinous crime.

Who is the head honcho here?

It couldn't be Sam Hart. He had patrolled the building, his back arched, the butt of his M16 against his chest, his entire body emanating nervous energy.

No, he was just another goon.

Who does he work for?

The more Tanya thought about it, the more Sheriff Reginald came to mind. He relished being the top dog and wielded his power any way he could. Of all the people in this town, he fit the bill the best.

After another scan around the living room to make sure no one was watching, she stepped up to the landing. A second staircase led to the top floor.

She gazed up at it, wanting more than anything to run up and find those kids. But she had to secure this floor so no one could attack her from behind while she carried out her rescue mission.

In the far end of the living room was what looked like a den. An office of sorts. The door was ajar. She couldn't see much or hear anything from inside, but her senses tingled.

There's someone in there. I just know it.

Tanya tiptoed along the wall, sticking to the shadows. If anyone stepped out of that office or came down the stairs, she would be a sitting target, but that was a risk she had to take.

When she was ten feet from the den, she heard a strange noise coming from inside. She stopped in her tracks and trained her ear.

Raspy breathing, followed by a low whimper.

Someone's inside.

The kids?

Her heart raced.

She stepped up to the door. She could hear the weeping clearly now, but something about it felt off. The quiet sobbing was mixed in with laborious breathing, like the person had been seriously injured.

This isn't a child.

Keeping her body shielded behind the wall, Tanya kicked the door open.

She took a sharp breath in.

Sam Hart.

Chapter Thirty-seven

At close quarters, Sam looked very much like his brother Eric.

And like his brother, Sam Hart had also been shot.

But Sam was still alive, trembling in pain, his eyes scrunched like he could barely manage his agony.

He was on the rug, his legs splayed out, leaning against an armchair, his right hand clutching his stomach. That didn't stop the blood from seeping out of the bullet wound and spreading across his hands and shirt.

But that wasn't what Tanya was focused on.

Strapped to the man's chest was a pipe bomb.

With shaking hands, Tanya pulled her phone out, and dialed. "Asha!"

"We're on our way out," came her friend's voice, sounding like she was in an echo chamber.

"Where are you?"

"In the tunnel."

"Did you close the vault door?"

"Yes. It's shut. Didn't want anyone to see us. I left Blake for the paramedics."

"Forget Blake." Tanya gritted her teeth. "You and Liam need to get to the end of the tunnel now. Don't come out of the bomb shelter until I tell you. Got it?"

"What's going on?"

"IED on first floor. Stay underground!"

Asha took a sharp breath in. "Copy that."

Tanya hung up, her heart racing, sweat pouring from her forehead.

Inside the den, Sam Hart whimpered louder, like he was vying for her attention. His breath was getting raspier with every passing second.

That scream she'd heard only moments ago had to have been him.

Who shot him?

"Don't move one inch," said Tanya as she peered down at the device on his chest.

Sam opened his mouth to speak, but couldn't seem to get the words out. He gurgled.

She leaned over him. "Who put this on you?"

He started to shake.

"Calm down, for heaven's sake." Tanya put a firm hand on his shoulder. "Stay still unless you want to blow yourself up."

He turned a terrified face to her and blinked rapidly, but his hands were still trembling. That was when she saw the countdown timer, partially hidden by his elbow.

Her eyes widened in shock.

Twenty-one minutes!

Her brain swirled like a tsunami.

Her training on explosive devices at Quantico had been superficial. Her days in the raw combat field were what would help her now. While she had never disarmed a bomb herself, she had watched others do it.

Focus, girl, focus.

She crouched to take a better look.

It was a crude homemade device, tied around Sam's chest with a loose cable. That meant whoever did this was an amateur or had been in a major hurry. Either scenario only escalated the risks exponentially.

Tanya's eyes flashed over to the timer.

Twenty minutes.

She couldn't depend on that. The explosion could happen at any moment. The stories of premature detonation of homemade explosives were too many to ignore.

"Help me," whimpered Sam. "Please, help me."

She leaned in closer to scrutinize the end caps of the pipe, when a loud bang made her jump. She sprang to her feet and whirled around, her heart pounding like mad.

Another bomb?

It took her panicked mind a few seconds to realize a crew had crashed through the bunker's main door and were hollering at each other.

It sounded like an army had descended inside.

The FBI?

Or someone else?

Chapter Thirty-eight

Tanya crept toward the den's open doorway, her Glock aimed forward.

Sheriff Reginald?

He was by the front entrance, shouting orders, and pointing all over the place. The four deputies who had crashed inside were swiveling around, their sidearms aimed at every corner of the hall, looking as confused as he was.

Tanya stepped outside of the den.

"Freeze!" shouted a deputy.

"Stone!" yelled the sheriff. "What the hell's going on?"

"You tell me," snarled Tanya. "Do you know what's inside this room?"

"Put your weapon down!" he shouted, his face turning red in anger.

"There's a pipe bomb strapped to Sam Hart's chest. This building will blow up in less than twenty minutes."

The sheriff's eyebrows shot up.

No one spoke.

The sheriff stepped up to her, his eyes darting back and forth, his weapon ready in his hand, like he was unsure if she was bluffing.

Tanya pushed the den's door fully open.

He stopped in his tracks, his eyes bulging. One look at the bleeding man huddled by her feet and his face turned white.

He stood frozen, while his crew stared at Sam Hart, terror etched on their faces.

Tanya holstered her weapon, realizing they were as stunned as she had been.

"There are four kids on the second floor. We have to get them out now. Blake's in the basement. He's injured."

"What on earth is going on, here?" said the sheriff, shock in his voice.

"Eveline was tracking those missing kids for a reason. Her husband and Pat's husband were running a pedophile streaming service. Their filming studio is in the basement." Tanya paused. "Deputy Blake was their henchman. He's down there right now, waiting for you to arrest him."

The sheriff gawked at her like he couldn't believe his ears.

Tanya didn't have time for this. There was a more urgent matter at hand.

She turned to the deputies.

"Do any of you know how to defuse a pipe bomb?"

They stared back at her, mute and immobile.

She cursed under her breath.

"Get the kids out!" she hollered. "On the second floor. Get them out before this building blows up!"

The sheriff suddenly seemed to come to life. He spun around to his men. "You heard her. Get Blake and the kids! Do it! Now!"

The deputies jumped to action. Two raced up the stairs and the other two dashed down to the basement.

The sheriff glanced at Sam Hart on the ground, his face flushed. "Is he still alive?"

"He won't be for long if he doesn't get medical aid soon," said Tanya.

The sheriff pointed at the bomb on his chest, his face flushed. "You know how to stop that thing?"

"I'm going to give it a try."

Her job had always been to protect the person defusing the bomb, not watch over their shoulder while they did their job. With enemy fire raging around, fighter jets roaring above, and potential snipers targeting her crew, her focus had been elsewhere.

Tanya's back was drenched in sweat. Adrenaline pounded through her veins again.

On the second floor, she could hear the running footsteps of the officers as they searched for the children. From down in the basement came the hollers of the men who had gone to rescue Blake.

"Please tell me they trained you guys on these," came the sheriff's anxious voice from behind her.

Tanya stared at the device.

Four wires, sheathed in brown plastic, seemed to connect to the detonator. The explosive mixture was most probably gunpowder. There could even be nails inside to inflict greater damage, though the device was too small to hold more than a fist full.

She narrowed her eyes.

Before they started deploying small robots to do the dangerous work, she had seen bomb experts cut the wires by hand.

But which ones?

She examined the end caps. If she could remove the fuse without triggering the...

Is that even possible? How the hell am I going to do this?

Tanya clenched her jaw. She had no idea how to save Sam. What she knew was that if this thing went off, the shrapnel would instantly kill anyone within two hundred yards.

She glanced at the timer.

Seventeen minutes.

"Please don't leave me," whimpered Sam Hart, his pleading eyes filled with tears.

"Stop moving."

Behind her, the sheriff's crew hollered at each other to hurry.

"Go! Go! Go!"

She glanced over her shoulder quickly to see them hustle two lanky boys toward the front door. The children stumbled out like zombies. She hoped to everything there were no more prisoners hidden in this hellhole.

"Can you do it?" came the sheriff's voice. "Or do we get out?"

Shut up. I'm trying to think.

One alternative was to stop the timer, but that didn't look possible. Another option would be to remove the device from Sam altogether, but that increased the risk of the explosive going off by an order of magnitude she didn't even want to calculate.

Tanya moved Sam's bloodied hands away from his stomach to get a closer look. A surprised shout from behind her made her stop in mid action.

"What in heaven's name are *you* doing here?" came the sheriff's angry voice. "Put that down!"

Chapter Thirty-nine

Tanya whirled around.

Hudson Wyatt stood on the threshold of the small side door.

His shoulders were relaxed, and he had a pleasant expression on his face, like he was coming over for a picnic lunch. But in his hands was the automatic rifle she had seen Sam carry with him during his patrol.

"Hello Reginald." Wyatt waved at the sheriff. "You followed the crumbs, I see. Thanks for coming."

"Hudson?" The sheriff looked dumbfounded. "What are you doing here?"

"Welcome to my humble business venture. I would have mentioned it earlier, but I knew how you would have reacted."

The sheriff's eyes bulged. "What are you saying? Are you part of this sick business? Did you take over? How...? How could you?"

"I've been trying to find the best way to get you in here today, and those out-of-town girls gave me the perfect idea."

Tanya's eyebrows shot up.

But she didn't have time for that puzzle.

She needed to figure out how to diffuse the explosive ASAP, but Wyatt was a wild card. He hadn't brought that gun in here for fun. With or without the pipe bomb going off, everybody could die in the next few seconds.

The sheriff was spluttering.

"Why on earth would you be involved in something like this? We... we went fishing together. Your sister and I—"

"For all your blustering, you're a sad, weak man, Reginald."

"Is this some sick game, Hudson?"

"I only play serious games. You'll die today, Reginald, but not to worry," Wyatt's smile widened, "this illustrious bunker will be your personal coffin."

"There's a bomb in here!" shouted Tanya. "This will be a coffin for all of us!"

Wyatt chuckled.

I should have known.

Tanya raised her hand and aimed the Glock at his chest.

Wyatt swung his weapon on her.

"I knew you'd come here with your friend. Thanks for making my life easier."

Tanya's heart raced as she considered the options. She could shoot him, but he could pull the trigger and spark a massacre inside the bunker.

"Don't worry," Wyatt was saying. "I'll get your other pal and your pup next. I know they're hiding in the woods, but they won't be for long—"

"Hudson Wyatt!" shouted the sheriff. His face had turned purple, like it was about to explode all on its own. "Stop this sick game right now! Put your weapon down!"

Wyatt turned toward him. That was the moment of distraction Tanya needed.

She fired, just as the sheriff barreled toward Wyatt.

Wyatt dove to the floor.

Her bullet ricocheted on the wall and fell to the ground.

She hurtled behind the den's door, her heart pounding.

Wyatt couldn't shoot in here.

He wouldn't.

A single bullet could trigger the explosive on Sam's chest and they would all die.

He wouldn't dare.

Or would he?

On the floor, Wyatt pulled the trigger on his automatic rifle.

A thundering rat-a-tat-tat cut across the hall. Bullets sprayed everywhere. Glass tables shattered, chairs overturned, and books were sent spinning into the air.

Tanya scrambled toward the couch on her stomach.

She crouched behind the armchair, her hands clutched over her head, her heart and mind pounding as she wondered if this was a suicide mission.

A stifled cry came from somewhere in the main room, followed by a thundering crash.

Sheriff Reginald!

Tanya's heart hammered in her chest.

Did Wyatt just kill the sheriff?

Suddenly, the gunfire died down. Just as abruptly as it had begun.

She held her breath.

Silence had fallen in the hall.

Tanya peeked out from behind the couch.

Without a warning, a single gunshot echoed through the room. She jerked her head back. Sam Hart let out a piercing screech.

His body convulsed.

He fell back against the armchair, his mouth open in a silent scream.

Sam Hart was dead.

But the bomb on his chest was still ticking.

Chapter Forty

A door slammed shut.

Tanya glanced around the armchair.

She couldn't see a thing except for Sam Hart's bloodied body lying against the couch.

It was a miracle the bomb hadn't gone off. But now was not the time to count her blessings.

Tanya leaped up and stepped up to the open doorway. She peeked outside the den, her weapon trained forward.

Wyatt had disappeared.

She scanned the hall. It looked like a tornado had ripped through the space, tossing furniture, breaking glass, and shattering the wood panels.

Where's the sheriff?

A groan came from behind the bullet-ridden bar. She ran over. Sheriff Reginald was writhing on the floor next to the counter, one hand clutching his left shoulder.

"Help!" he called out as he saw her. "I jumped in here but the bastard still got me."

She pulled him to a seated position and examined the open wound on his upper arm.

"Grazed," she said. "You'll lose some blood, but you're going to live."

Holding on to her, the sheriff got shakily to his feet.

"If I see that son of a—"

Tanya shook him by the shoulder. "We need to get out now."

"Wh... what about Sam?"

"Dead."

The sheriff stared at her in shock.

"Wyatt was trying to get me. He hit Sam instead."

"Geez—"

"If that bomb isn't a sham, this place will blow up in a few minutes."

She dragged him through the front door, her heart racing, wondering how much time they had till this entire structure collapsed.

She pulled on the sheriff's arm. "Run!"

He seemed to gain a second wind.

He scurried toward the woods behind her.

From somewhere in the distance, Tanya could hear the yells of the officers but couldn't see the squad cars.

"Where's your team?" she asked as they dashed into the tree line.

"Parked by your Jeep." The sheriff pointed a shaky hand. "That way."

Tanya only stopped running once they were well inside the woods. The hefty pine and fir trunks surrounding them would provide some protection from the blast, but it wouldn't be safe to hang around here.

She let go of the sheriff's arm. He staggered but kept his balance.

"Go to your crew. Get a medic to look at you," said Tanya. "My friend's still underground. I have to get her and the kid out."

"But—"

"Go!"

She whipped around and dashed through the trees in the direction of the hatch.

Behind her, she heard a loud rustling, like a rhinoceros was chasing her. She swung around to see the sheriff stumble after her, one hand still clutching his injured arm.

"I'm coming...," he shouted.

Ignoring him, Tanya kept running. He was a burden and would only slow her down.

Her heart pounded hard. Her nerves were wrecked as she expected to hear a blast from the bomb go off at any minute.

I'm coming, Asha.

She swung around a tree when she spotted the clearing.

Almost there.

She crossed her fingers.

Please be okay.

She dashed into the clearing and halted. She stood in place, panting, her eyes wide in shock.

She wasn't alone.

Standing in the middle of the clearing was Wyatt, his weapon still in his hands.

Next to him stood Pat and the little girl she had rescued from the shelter in the woods.

Noel.

Chapter Forty-one

P at was holding the girl by her spindly arm.

The woman's face was expressionless, and she no longer had her cane.

A dark scowl had replaced Wyatt's smug smile. Tanya could see he hadn't expected her to get out of the building or to run into him here.

Noel was in a hospital gown, her face even paler than before. *How did they get her out?*

The girl shot Tanya a terrified glance from under her lashes.

Tanya wanted to call out to her, but she was trembling like a frightened lamb headed to a slaughterhouse. She knew one wrong move on her part could mean life or death for Noel.

Where's Asha and Liam? Are they safe?

She scanned the hatch. It was still closed. The worst possibilities swirled through her mind like a category five hurricane. She prayed her friend and the kid were still inside and wouldn't come out.

Not now.

Sheriff Reginald caught up to her and stood behind her, breathing down her neck, panting loudly. But Tanya didn't dare turn her eyes away from Wyatt.

He had tried to kill them once. He would try again.

Before she could do anything, the sheriff shoved her aside and limped forward.

"Hudson!" he roared. "You bastard! You shot at me!"

Tanya glanced at him from the side of her eyes. His face was red with fury. He glowered at his brother-in-law and swayed on his feet like a drunkard.

"Is this how you can afford the Jaguar and your oceanfront property?"

"What I can afford and how are none of your damned business," snapped Wyatt.

"It is my business when you break the damn law!"

Tanya kept a close watch on where Wyatt's gun was pointing.

"You've been running a child porn ring!" shouted the sheriff. "You live on blood money!"

"My family's wealthy," snarled Wyatt. "You know that, Reginald."

The sheriff's mouth curled in contempt.

"I know all about your money trouble. Your sister's my wife, remember?" He shook his head. "How could you? I trusted you."

"You may have a sheriff's badge, but you're no better than a city beat cop. My family never forgave my sister for marrying beneath us. She always had bad judgment."

The sheriff spluttered, like he couldn't get his words out.

"She erased seven decades of profit in only three years," said Wyatt. "Just like that my family will lose everything. All because of her."

The sheriff's eyes widened. "She runs a legitimate business! How could you get involved in something like *this*?"

"Someone had to help out when Tom died."

Wyatt turned to Pat and laughed a hollow laugh.

Pat didn't respond. She was observing them carefully, her face stoic.

Tanya had a flashback to Cora's Café. Pat had remained in her corner, watching the aftermath of the murder-suicide with more curiosity than horror.

She has no heart.

"This is a lucrative operation," Wyatt was saying. "We make money hand over fist. These kids are our golden geese. It's more profitable than what my dumb sister's eking out of our family business."

"You hurt children!" shouted the sheriff.

Wyatt screwed his eyes.

"You're a small man with a small mind. You put your hours in and go fishing on weekends. Me, I built a global enterprise."

The sheriff shook his head. "What's your sister going to think when she finds out?"

Wyatt's face darkened.

"My family's company should have come to me!" he shouted. "I was the smart one. But my father gave it all to my stupid sister, and look where that got us!"

He spoke with such venom, the sheriff stepped back.

"That's my wife you're talking about!"

Stop it. Tanya scolded the sheriff in her mind. He was riling up a man who held the power to execute them all in a matter of seconds.

Wyatt spat to the side. "She's as empty headed and power hungry as you are. All I wanted, all my life, was to stick it to her. She lost. I won."

"You're a psychopathic criminal!" yelled the sheriff.

Pat snapped at those words.

"We're businesspeople!" she shouted, making Noel jump in fright.

"You too, Pat?" The sheriff's face turned pale. "How could you be involved in this sick game?"

Pat glared at the sheriff, her eyes like laser beams, like she could burn him into ashes.

Tanya's head cleared as the last puzzle pieces fell into place.

Pat and Wyatt had been playing with them all along.

She stepped forward, her finger on the trigger and her Glock aimed at the ground, but ready to whip it up at a moment's notice.

"Now I know why you both came to talk to us," she said. "You dropped hints about this place. You wanted us in the bunker when it blew up, didn't you?"

Wyatt didn't answer but Pat blinked.

Tanya turned to her.

"You took over from your husband after he died. You run this show, don't you, Pat?"

The sheriff cursed and glared at his brother-in-law.

"What does that make you, then? Business partner of a kiddie porn ring? You'll go straight to hell, Hudson. You'll never get away with this."

"You forget it's *you* who's cornered," said Wyatt, gripping his gun tighter.

The instant Tanya saw Wyatt lift his arm, she whipped up her Glock and pulled the trigger. Straight between his eyes. The automatic rifle flew out of his hand and slammed against a tree.

Noel screamed.

Wyatt dropped to the dirt with a groan.

Tanya sprang forward and grabbed his gun. When she spun around, she saw the sheriff's hands up, his face clouded in fear.

Pat was holding a revolver, and she was aiming it at him.

Tanya fired her Glock before Pat could react.

The woman fell with a shriek.

That was when the explosion rocked the ground.

"Down!" Tanya grabbed Noel and pulled her behind the trees. Sheriff Reginald lunged toward them.

"Heads down!" he hollered as they all crashed to the forest floor.

A second and third blast followed the first. Then came the thundering roar of the bunker collapsing, shaking the ground like an earthquake had hit the area.

Tanya held on to Noel and kept her head down, her mind whirring.

There had been more than one explosive in the building. All the evidence of Pat and Wyatt's criminal activities was now buried under a massive rubble together with the bloodied remains of Sam Hart.

A familiar sound came from up above the tree canopy.

A chopper.

Tanya raised her head.

A black helicopter came into view over the treetops briefly, before tilting and disappearing from her sight.

FBI.

Tanya let out a breath.

Special Agent in Charge Desmond had read her messages, after all.

Her phone rang. She yanked it out of her pocket.

"Asha! Are you okay?"

Day Three

Chapter Forty-two

Asha took a sip of her hot Ceylon tea and leaned back in her patio chair.

Katy pulled her chocolate caramel latte toward her.

"I knew something was wrong with Wyatt," said Katy, picking up a long spoon to scoop up the whipped cream. "I suspected him from the beginning."

Tanya and Asha stared at their friend.

"You were gawking at his house, his car, even his dog," said Tanya. "If I hadn't shooed him off, you'd be lying dead in his house by now."

"You can't trust everyone you meet, Katy," said Asha. *"Especially* when they flash shiny things your way."

The three of them were sitting next to a pile of wood that used to be the patio for Cora's Corner Café.

The front of the shop had been boarded up and looked like a construction site, but the kitchen had remained untouched. Cora had set a rattan table and a handful of chairs on the grass outside.

"Pat fooled us all," said Katy. "Admit it. Even you two thought she was legitimately innocent."

"She was a smart one, I'll give you that," said Tanya, stroking Max who was sleeping by her feet. "After she took over from her dead husband, she hired Wyatt to bring in the wealthy clients. She had the business. He had the connections."

"She hated Noel for taking her husband's attention away from her," said Asha. "Can you imagine being jealous of your own adopted daughter? A kid who was being abused? If there's a hell, I hope she gets a one-way ticket to it."

"Along with Wyatt, Tom, and Eveline's husband," said Tanya.

They had just returned from the hospital, where the FBI's Violent Crimes Against Children program had taken Noel and the three boys for a medical and psychological checkup.

The program would decide on their next steps. There was nothing more they could do than let due process play out.

But Noel had clung to Tanya and Liam to Asha, even when the hospital staff insisted that visiting hours were over. After promising the kids they would return, Tanya, Asha, and Katy had come over to Cora's Café to collect their thoughts.

They were still reeling over what had happened in the bunker in the woods. It felt like a strange dream, a terrifying nightmare they couldn't shake off.

"Eveline Hart was a good person," said Asha. "The world needs more people like her."

Tanya looked at her friend.

"She murdered her own son."

"That was a crime of passion," said Asha. "I saw her through the window. Her eyes were blazing in fury and horror. She had no choice but to end it all, right there and then."

"I know why she hid her family photos now," said Katy. "They reminded her of a time that no longer existed. Her family was causing her unspeakable grief, but she didn't want to throw the old photos away either. So, she hid them. I'd have done the same in her shoes."

"I can only imagine the anguish she must have gone through," said Asha, shaking her head. "Poor woman."

Tanya studied her coffee cup.

"It's her husband's and Tom's deaths I'm more interested in," she said. "I'm willing to put my money on induced heart attacks, which would mean cold-blooded murder. Potentially carried out by Eveline Hart."

"How do you know?" said Katy, sitting up. "Do you have any evidence to say that?"

"It's a gut feel. Their deaths weren't natural." Tanya shrugged. "We'll never know, unless the sheriff gives the green light to exhume their bodies and do an autopsy. There's no career glory or political reward in that, so I doubt he'll ever reopen those cold cases."

"Those two men were psychopaths." Katy said gloomily to her half-drunk latte cup. "If Eveline killed them off, they deserved to die."

"Imagine how much pain she went through when she learned what her husband was up to," said Asha. "A man she probably loved and trusted at one point. She was trying to right terrible wrongs, the only way she knew how."

Tanya put her coffee down.

Was there ever a justification for murder? In her youth, she would have yelled out a resounding yes. But now, she wasn't so sure.

She stared at the half-eaten chocolate cookie in front of her, her appetite gone.

While no one was bringing it up, she had done her own killings in the woods. Wyatt and Pat had died instantly, and she would have to live with the knowledge she had taken two more lives.

Tanya had killed criminals before, but each one of the evil men and women she had removed from earth came to haunt her at night.

She rubbed her tired eyes.

"More coffee?"

They looked up to see Cora step out of the kitchen door. She walked over to them with a pot of freshly brewed coffee and a bowl of water for Max.

Her eyes were lined and her face was haggard, like she had aged several years over the past few days. No one in Paradise Cove had been immune to the ghastly discovery at the bunker. It was like the entire town had plunged into mourning.

Cora placed the water bowl next to Max with a tired smile. Max wagged his tail and got up to drink.

"Good boy," she said, patting his back. "I hear you're getting your cone removed today."

"Can't wait," said Tanya, watching her pup lapping the bowl, spraying water all over the place. "He's been whining about it. I hope he'll forgive me one day."

Cora straightened up and filled Tanya's coffee cup without asking. Then, with a heavy sigh, she set the pot down and turned her troubled face to the three women.

"You girls were so brave. I don't know how you did it, but I'm glad you saved those children."

She wiped her eyes.

"Blake was my sister-in-law's son. He coached baseball at the high school and volunteered at the Salvation Army every Christmas. How did I not know he was living a double life?" She sighed. "And Pat? Of all people. She was my friend! How could I have not known?"

Katy put a hand on Cora's arm.

"Why don't you close shop and take a week off. Come back when they've rebuilt the café. That way, you won't have this reminder of what happened staring you in the face."

Cora shook her head.

"I need to stay busy. Keeps my mind off the bad things. My café means everything to me."

She gazed into the distance.

"In a strange way, it feels a little lighter around here. Like there was a heavy cloud hanging over this town for years, but it's gone now."

"You can't blame yourself for what Blake or Pat did," said Asha, "or for not seeing what was going on. No one knew. Not even the sheriff."

Cora picked up her coffee pot.

"I know you gals are trying to make me feel better, and I appreciate that." She smiled a small smile and turned to leave. Then, as if she remembered something, she whirled around.

"Before I forget, Sheriff Reginald's recovering well."

Tanya grimaced. He had redeemed himself in the end, but she never wanted to deal with the man again.

"Doctors are still monitoring him, but I hear he's ordering everyone around from his hospital bed."

"Why am I not surprised?" said Tanya.

With a friendly wave, Cora disappeared inside her café.

Asha turned to Katy.

"Hurry and finish your latte. Our flight leaves in an hour and we still have to get to the airport."

"I'll drive you over," said Tanya.

"Let me go pay," said Asha, picking up her teacup.

"I need the washroom," announced Katy, as she followed her friend inside the café.

Tanya cracked open her water bottle to fill up Max's bowl, when her phone rang. She slipped it out of her pocket and stared at the screen.

Restricted.

Her heart skipped a beat.

She hadn't talked to her boss after what had happened. While all had ended well, she had broken so many rules, she was sure her career with the bureau was over.

She accepted the call and braced herself.

"Stone here."

"Agent Tanya Stone?" came a sharp male voice.

That's not Paul Desmond.

"Director Beatrix Cross wants to talk to you."

Tanya pulled her chair back and stood up, as if the director herself was in front of her.

"Did you say Direc—"

The assistant cut her off. "I'm putting you through now."

Tanya's heart sank.

I'm so fired.

She heard a click. Then the FBI director's voice came on the line.

"I heard what you did in Paradise Cove. You've been busy."

Tanya's heart raced.

"Yes, ma'am."

"Sheriff Reginald called us from the hospital."

Tanya closed her eyes.

This is it.

"He thanked us for your help."

Tanya snapped her eyes open.

"He appreciates your support in bringing down the child porn ring."

A slight flush crept up Tanya's neck.

Support? We did all the work.

"He said your cooperation was stellar, and that you helped his team close the case."

Tanya shook her head.

So Sheriff Reginald was taking all the credit. Just like him.

"We need that report on the two civilians who were shot by the bunker. Pronto."

"I'm on it," Tanya blurted. "It will be on Agent Desmond's desk tonight."

"Send it directly to me."

Tanya's eyebrows shot up.

The reporting lines within the bureau were extensive and sometimes complicated, but you never went over your boss's head. That was, unless you wanted to get ostracized by your colleagues for the rest of your career.

But did she have a choice?

"Will do, ma'am."

"I have a new case for you."

"I'm ready," said Tanya, recalling her earlier conversation with Desmond.

"Black Rock. A small seaside town an hour south of Seattle. You'll be going undercover as a contractor to the local police chief's office."

"Roger that."

"The chief is new to town and new to the job. Name's Jack Bold. Desmond will send you details later today."

"I would like to take Max with me."

"Affirmative. As long as the vet gives the all-clear."

"What's the mission's goal, ma'am?"

"Over the past five years, we've had reports of a series of unsolved murders along the coast. All remain unresolved. Serious crime rates have been steadily increasing along the coastal front. They haven't received national press yet, but we're tracking them."

"The work of a serial killer?" said Tanya.

"Perhaps. Could be organized crime. What I need right now is boots on the ground, watching, listening, and reporting back."

"Copy that."

"I knew I could depend on you. Your combat experience gives you a leg up. Glad to have you on board, Stone."

Tanya blinked.

Did she really say that?

"I'm usually fire fighting jurisdictional issues," came Cross's voice. "It's nice to see us cooperating with the local precincts and getting results for a change. Reginald said his office will give you a commendation. Good job, Agent."

Cross hung up before Tanya could even digest that last bit of news. She stared at her phone.

A commendation?

She shook her head to clear it.

Forget the sheriff and his games. I have more important things to do now.

A thrill went through her as she realized she was about to embark on her first solo mission, a rarity for a recruit.

She turned to Max with a wide grin.

"You and me are off to our first FBI mission, bud," she said, ruffling his ears.

Max thumped his tail on the ground and licked her hand.

Tanya's smile widened.

It was good to be on the road again.

She touched her sunflower pendant and thanked her mother for watching over her. She never lived to see her grow up, but she knew she'd be proud of her.

"Black Rock," Tanya whispered to herself. "Here we come."

⊷———⊶

Thank you for reading HER DEADLY END. I hope you enjoyed this story.

Would you like to read the epilogue story? A year later, Tanya, Asha, Katy, and Max return to Paradise Cove for a weekend to visit the children and see how they're faring. They make a shocking discovery about the sheriff and learn how the two men—Pat and Eveline's husbands—were killed.

And by whom.

It's not who you think it is....

Get the twisty bonus epilogue here. Paradise Cove Twist https://books.tikiriherath.com/ts-paradisecovetwistsold

⊷———⊶

Want more spine-tingling mystery thrillers with Tanya and Max?

HER COLD BLOOD is the next book in this series.

Nothing in Black Rock is what it seems. The serial killer could be anyone. He could be standing right behind you...

Turn the page to start reading the next book right here!

Continue the adventure with *Her Cold Blood*

Chapter One – ESCAPE TO DEATH

❖━━❖

His heavy footsteps thundered on the concrete floor.

Laura's blood chilled.

Her small naked feet propelled her forward. It was like they had a life of their own.

She didn't realize she was leaving trails of blood in her wake, like breadcrumbs for him to follow.

His footsteps got louder.

Terror coursed through her veins. Her heart beat so hard she was sure it would explode inside her rib cage.

She wasn't going back to that dank basement, where she'd get strapped down like an animal to be butchered.

No!

Laura raced through the whitewashed corridors of the eerie underground maze that smelled like a slaughterhouse. She passed the ominous red door, but didn't dare look that way.

Behind that door was where the nightmares began. Ones you could never escape from. Laura's mind spun like the head of an exorcist doll, mad memories exploding like fireworks.

She had to get out.

Now!

Keep running.

The fluorescent light fixtures on the bare ceiling flickered and buzzed sharply. It was like they were signaling her position to her captor.

Faster!

He was getting close, stomping down the stairs, calling her name. A second familiar voice hollered after him. Laura's heart sank.

Is she after me, too?

A loud plop sounded on the wall beside her. The white plaster exploded into a thousand pieces and sprayed the corridor, stinging her bare arms and thighs.

Another plop.

She ducked.

The wall plaster sprayed over her like gun shrapnel. She covered her head.

He's shooting at me!

She glanced back, her heart racing, her eyes wild with horror, expecting to spot him at the other end. The corridor was empty, but the footsteps were getting close.

He's shooting blindly. He doesn't know where I am.

She opened her right palm and looked at the crumpled paper she'd been clutching. *Quick.* She stuffed it into her mouth.

If they find me dead, they'll know who did it.

Laura spun around and rocketed through the corridor, trying hard not to make a sound.

Almost there.

She reached the door at the end of the tunnel. She grabbed the handle and turned it forcefully.

The force of the heavy basement door hurled her backward. Bright sunlight streamed through the narrow steps, blinding her, but she didn't have one second to lose.

She flew up the steps, her chest heaving. She didn't hear the steel basement door clang shut behind her.

She halted at the top and blinked, disoriented.

Rows of roses burst in colors next to a manicured cedar hedge. Tall, stately trees lined the perimeter, like giant sentinels shielding the house from the rest of the world.

From afar, she could hear waves crash against the shore below. She wasn't far from the Black Rock cliffs.

Her eyes darted back and forth, desperate to find an escape. That was when she noticed the wall that ran along the property line.

Her heart sank.

She was trapped.

Again.

There was only one thing to do now.

She leaped toward the closest tree and grabbed the lowest branch. Holding on, she scrambled up the oak trunk like a monkey.

She clambered higher and higher on her wobbly legs, ignoring the rough bark scraping her bare skin, propelled by her will to live.

She was halfway up when the basement door banged open.

She froze and squinted through the leafy foliage.

They're here!

224

She turned and peered over the wall.

Freedom.

The hiking trail was down below. The path she'd walked only a few days ago, before he seized her and....

Think! What do I do now?

The massive oak tree spread over the enclosure, giving shade to the trail outside. Clinging to a branch, she inched toward the wall.

"Laura! Get down right now!" came a furious male voice. "Get down or I'll shoot to kill!"

But Laura wasn't listening to him anymore. She treaded on, clutching whatever she could. Her entire body was trembling so much, she was scared her hands would slip, but one thing kept her moving.

He's lying.

He needed her alive. He hated spilling even one ounce of precious blood. That's why he had fired his weapon near her. Not at her.

She teetered over the wall, ignoring the angry shouting below.

The bough bowed dangerously with her weight. It was too thin at the end.

The branch snapped with a loud crack. Laura fell through the air, barely feeling her T-shirt rip against a sharp twig.

The cold air rushed against her face.

She heard an ugly thump, followed by a searing pain that scorched through her frail body. Her head hammered like an army battalion had stormed inside and was firing machine guns.

She tried to open her eyes, but all she could see was a blur of blinking stars. She flexed her hands and touched something crumbly.

Dirt.

A dog barked nearby.

Someone was shouting. She didn't recognize the voice.

Help. Please. Help me. Her cries were deafening inside her head, but her throat refused to work.

The barking was muffled, but so close.

Laura tried to raise her head, but she couldn't move.

A dog barked again.

Wait.

It was an entire *pack* of dogs.

To be continued...

﹅━━━﹅

HER COLD BLOOD: A gripping crime thriller with a jaw-dropping twist.

Continue reading HER COLD BLOOD here: Tanya Stone FBI K9 Mystery Thrillers

www.TikiriHerath.com/Thrillers

And find out how to get early access to all the books in the Tanya Stone FBI K9 series.

﹅━━━﹅

HER COLD BLOOD

I'll take a pound of flesh and all your blood....

A spate of deadly crimes has paralyzed the secluded small town of Black Rock. Girls are vanishing without a trace.

New FBI recruit, Agent Tanya Stone's first case is to hunt the cold-blooded killer prowling the West Coast. With her K9 partner, she has one chance to prove her worth and keep the job she desperately needs.

When she stumbles across a dead girl in a ditch and the shocking photo of a torture room, she vows to unmask the psychopath's identity. Even if it risks her own life.

But dark and twisted secrets seethe underneath the perfect lives of this upscale neighborhood. The monster lives among them, spreading vicious lies.

Nothing in Black Rock is what it seems.

The serial killer could be anyone. He could be standing right behind you...

◆————◆

Continue reading HER COLD BLOOD: Tanya Stone FBI K9 Mystery Thrillers
www.TikiriHerath.com/Thrillers

Get your thriller fix! And find out how to get early access to all the books in the Tanya Stone FBI K9 series.

◆————◆

Available in e-book, paperback, and hardback editions in all good bookstores. Also available for free in libraries everywhere. Just ask your friendly local librarian to order a copy via Ingram Spark.

There is no graphic violence, heavy cursing, or explicit sex in these books. No dog is harmed in this story, but the villains are.

Author's Note

D ear friend,

Did you enjoy this novel?

My promise is to give you an exciting escape with every book I write, and I sure hope I have done so.

If you have a minute, would you leave an honest review of this book on Goodreads, Bookbub, or any of the online bookstores? Just one sentence would do.

Honest reader reviews help get my books selected for international promotions and I get to reach more readers around the world. Thank you from the bottom of my heart!

Have you heard of The Rebel Reader Club?

My reader club is a super fan community where you can get early access to my new books before anyone else in the world.

You will also have access to bonus true crime and K9 stories, fun swag like postcards, reader stickers, and bookmarks, bookish merchandise like signed paperbacks, and VIP tickets to *Tea with Tikiri,* and more.

And you get to decide what you want to be. A Detective, a Special Agent, or an FBI Director.

Click the link below to check out my reader club. You can read *Her Deadly End* for free too.
Come, join the fun and get your thriller fix!
https://reamstories.com/tikiri

See you on the inside.
My very best wishes,
Tikiri
Vancouver, Canada

PS/ Have you downloaded the epilogue of this book yet? Don't forget to get the bonus epilogue to this book. Asha, Katy, Tanya, and Max return to Paradise Cove a year later to visit the children and make a shocking new discovery.
Twisty Bonus Epilogue: Paradise Cove Twist
https://books.tikiriherath.com/ts-paradisecovetwistsold

PPS/ If you didn't enjoy the story or spotted typos, would you drop me a line and let me know? Or just write to say hello. I would love to hear from you and personally reply to every email I receive.
My email address is: Tikiri@TikiriHerath.com

The Reading List

The Red Heeled Rebels universe of mystery thrillers, featuring your favorite kick-ass female characters:

＊———・・——＊

Tanya Stone FBI K9 Mystery Thrillers
www.TikiriHerath.com/Thrillers
NEW FBI thriller series starring Tetyana from the Red Heeled Rebels as Special Agent Tanya Stone, and Max, as her loyal German Shepherd. These are serial killer thrillers set in Black Rock, a small upscale resort town on the coast of Washington state.
Her Deadly End
Her Cold Blood
Her Last Lie
Her Secret Crime
Her Perfect Murder
Her Grisly Grave

Asha Kade Private Detective Murder Mysteries
www.TikiriHerath.com/Mysteries
   Each book is a standalone murder mystery thriller, featuring the Red Heeled Rebels, Asha Kade and Katy McCafferty. Asha and Katy receive one million dollars for their favorite children's charity from a secret benefactor's estate every time they solve a cold case.
   Merciless Legacy
   Merciless Games
   Merciless Crimes
   Merciless Lies
   Merciless Past
   Merciless Deaths

Red Heeled Rebels International Mystery & Crime - The Origin Story
www.TikiriHerath.com/RedHeeledRebels
   The award-winning origin story of the Red Heeled Rebels characters. Learn how a rag-tag group of trafficked orphans from different places united to fight for their freedom and their lives, and became a found family.
   The Girl Who Crossed the Line
   The Girl Who Ran Away
   The Girl Who Made Them Pay
   The Girl Who Fought to Kill
   The Girl Who Broke Free

The Girl Who Knew Their Names
The Girl Who Never Forgot

◆———◆

The Accidental Traveler
www.TikiriHerath.com
An anthology of personal short stories based on the author's
sojourns around the world.

◆———◆

The Rebel Diva Nonfiction Series
www.TikiriHerath.com/Nonfiction
Your Rebel Dreams: 6 simple steps to take back control of your
life in uncertain times.

Your Rebel Plans: 4 simple steps to getting unstuck and making
progress today.

Your Rebel Life: Easy habit hacks to enhance happiness in the
10 key areas of your life.

Bust Your Fears: 3 simple tools to crush your anxieties and
squash your stress.

◆———◆

Collaborations
The Boss Chick's Bodacious Destiny Nonfiction Bundle
Dark Shadows 2: Voodoo and Black Magic of New Orleans

Tikiri's novels and nonfiction books are available on all good bookstores around the world.

These books are also available in libraries everywhere. Just ask your friendly local librarian or your local bookstore to order a copy via Ingram Spark.

www.TikiriHerath.com

Happy reading.

Debate this Dozen

Twelve Book Club Questions

1. Who was your favorite character?
2. Which characters did you dislike?
3. Which scene has stuck with you the most? Why?
4. What scenes surprised you?
5. What was your favorite part of the book?
6. What was your least favorite part?
7. Did any part of this book strike a particular emotion in you? Which part and what emotion did the book make you feel?
8. Did you know the author has written an underlying message in this story? What theme or life lesson do you think this story tells?
9. What did you think of the author's writing?
10. How would you adapt this book into a movie? Who would you cast in the leading roles?
11. On a scale of one to ten, how would you rate this story?
12. Would you read another book by this author?

Tanya Stone FBI K9 Mystery Thrillers

*H*ow far would you go to avenge your family's brutal murder?

Tanya Stone FBI K9 Serial Killer Thrillers

Her Deadly End
Her Cold Blood
Her Last Lie
Her Secret Crime
Her Perfect Murder
Her Grisly Grave

◆━━━◆

A brand-new FBI K9 serial killer thriller series for a pulse-pounding, bone-chilling adventure from the comfort and warmth of your favorite reading chair at home.

Can you find the killer before Agent Tanya Stone?

www.TikiriHerath.com/thrillers

◆———————◆

Some small-town secrets will haunt your nightmares. Escape if you can...

FBI Special Agent Tanya Stone has a new assignment. Hunt down the serial killers prowling the idyllic West Coast resort towns.

An unspeakable and bone-chilling darkness seethes underneath these picturesque seaside suburbs. A string of violent abductions and gruesome murders wreak hysteria among the perfect lives of the towns' families.

But nothing is what it seems. The monsters wear masks and mingle with the townsfolk, spreading vicious lies.

With her K9 German Shepherd, Agent Stone goes on the warpath. She will fight her own demons as a trafficked survivor to make the perverted psychopaths pay.

But now, they're after her.

Small towns have dark deceptions and sealed lips. If they know you know the truth, they'll never let you leave...

◆———————◆

Each book is a standalone murder mystery thriller, featuring Tetyana from the Red Heeled Rebels as Agent Tanya Stone, and Max, her loyal German Shepherd. Red Heeled Rebels Asha Kade and Katy McCafferty and their found family make guest appearances when Tanya needs help.

There is no graphic violence, heavy cursing, or explicit sex in these books.

The dogs featured in this series are never harmed, but the villains are.

———

To learn more about this exciting new series and find out how to get early access to all the books in the Tanya Stone FBI K9 series, go to www.TikiriHerath.com/thrillers
Sign up to Tikiri's Rebel Reader Club to get the chance to win personalized paperback books, chat with the author and more.

———

Available in e-book, paperback, and hardback editions on all good bookstores around the world. Print books are available for free in libraries everywhere. Just ask your friendly local librarian or your local bookstore to order a copy via Ingram Spark.

Asha Kade Private Detective Murder Mysteries

How far would you go for a million-dollar payout?

The Merciless Murder Mysteries

Merciless Legacy
Merciless Games
Merciless Crimes
Merciless Lies
Merciless Past
Merciless Deaths

◆———◆

Each book is a standalone murder mystery thriller featuring the Red Heeled Rebel, Asha Kade, and her best friend Katy

McCafferty, as private detectives on the hunt for serial killers in small towns USA.

There is no graphic violence, heavy cursing, or explicit sex in these books. What you will find are a series of suspicious deaths, a closed circle of suspects, twists and turns, fast-paced action, and nail-biting suspense.

www.TikiriHerath.com/mysteries

✦———✦

A newly minted private investigator, Asha Kade, gets a million dollars from an eccentric client's estate every time she solves a cold case. Asha Kade accepts this bizarre challenge, but what she doesn't bargain for is to be drawn into the dark underworld of her past again.

The only thing that propels her forward now is a burning desire for justice.

✦———✦

What readers are saying on Amazon and Goodreads:

"My new favorite series!"

"Thrilling twists, unputdownable!"

"I was hooked right from the start!"

"A twisted whodunnit! Edge of your seat thriller that kept me up late, to finish it, unputdownable!! More, please!"

"Buckle up for a roller coaster of a ride. This one will keep you on the edge of your seat."

"A must read! A macabre start to an excellent book. It had me totally gripped from the start and just got better!"

"A great whodunit with a lot of twists and turns along the way. The story was amazing!"

"I could not stop reading it. It was as if I was there witnessing the murders myself. The characters had depth and personality and backgrounds that were explained nicely. It was awesome!"

"Nothing is more terrifying than the fear of the unknown. Do you have any nails left? Another NAIL-BITING story from a very talented master storyteller!"

⊷————⊶

A brand-new murder mystery series for a pulse-pounding, bone-chilling adventure from the comfort and warmth of your favorite reading chair at home.

Can you find the killer before Asha Kade does?

⊷————⊶

To learn more about this exciting series, go to www.TikiriHerath.com/mysteries.
Sign up to Tikiri's Rebel Reader Club to get the chance to win personalized paperback books, chat with the author and more.

⊷————⊶

Available in e-book, paperback, and hardback editions on all good bookstores around the world. Print books are available for free in libraries everywhere. Just ask your friendly local librarian or your local bookstore to order a copy via Ingram Spark.

The Red Heeled Rebels International Mystery & Crime

The Origin Story

Would you like to know the origin story of your favorite characters in the Tanya Stone FBI K9 mystery thrillers and the Asha Kade Merciless murder mysteries?

In the award-winning Red Heeled Rebels international mystery & crime series—the origin story—you'll find out how Asha, Katy, and Tetyana (Tanya) banded together in their troubled youths to fight for freedom against all odds.

◆———→◆

The complete Red Heeled Rebels international crime collection:

Prequel Novella: The Girl Who Crossed the Line

Book One: The Girl Who Ran Away
Book Two: The Girl Who Made Them Pay
Book Three: The Girl Who Fought to Kill
Book Four: The Girl Who Broke Free
Book Five: The Girl Who Knew Their Names
Book Six: The Girl Who Never Forgot
The series is now complete!

◆———◆

An epic, pulse-pounding, international crime thriller series that spans four continents featuring a group of spunky, sassy young misfits who have only each other for family.

A multiple-award-winning series which would be best read in order. There is no graphic violence, heavy cursing, or explicit sex in these books.

www.TikiriHerath.com/RedHeeledRebels

◆———◆

In a world where justice no longer prevails, six iron-willed young women rally to seek vengeance on those who stole their humanity.

If you like gripping thrillers with flawed but strong female leads, vigilante action in exotic locales and twists that leave you at the edge of your seat, you'll love these books by multiple award-winning Canadian novelist, Tikiri Herath.

Go on a heart-pounding international adventure without having to get a passport or even buy an airline ticket!

◆———◆

What readers are saying on Amazon and Goodreads:

"Fast-paced and exciting!"

"An exciting and thought-provoking book."

"A wonderful story! I didn't want to leave the characters."

"I couldn't put down this exciting road trip adventure with a powerful message."

"Another award-worthy adventure novel that keeps you on the edge of your seat."

"A heart-stopping adventure. I just couldn't put the book down till I finished reading it."

"Kept me mesmerized and captivated with the rich descriptions which made me feel like I was actually inside the story."

"This is a fantastic read that will have you traveling the globe. I absolutely loved this book. You won't be able to put it down!"

"A real page-turner and international thriller. Reminds me of why I've always loved to read. Because I can visit worlds and places, I wouldn't ordinarily get to see."

❖——•——❖

Literary Awards & Praise for The Red Heeled Rebels books:

- Grand Prize Award Finalist - 2019 Eric Hoffer Award, USA

- First Horizon Award Finalist - 2019 Eric Hoffer Award, USA

- Honorable Mention General Fiction - 2019 Eric Hoffer Award, USA

- Winner First-In-Category - 2019 Chanticleer Somerset Award, USA

- Semi-Finalist - 2020 Chanticleer Somerset Award, USA

- Winner in 2019 Readers' Favorite Book Awards, USA

- Winner of 2019 Silver Medal - Excellence E-Lit Award, USA

- Winner in Suspense Category - 2018 New York Big Book Award, USA

- Finalist in Suspense Category - 2018 & 2019 Silver Falchion Awards, USA

- Honorable Mention - 2018-19 Reader Views Literary Classics Award, USA

- Publisher's Weekly Booklife Prize - 2018, USA

＋―――――＋

To learn more about this addictive series, go to **www.TikiriHerath.com/RedHeeledRebels** and receive the prequel novella - **The Girl Who Crossed The Line** - as a gift.

Sign up to Tikiri's Rebel Reader club and get bonus stories, exotic recipes, the chance to win paperbacks, chat with the author and more.

＋―――――＋

Available in e-book, paperback, and hardback editions on all good bookstores around the world. Print books are available for free in libraries everywhere. Just ask your friendly local librarian or your local bookstore to order a copy via Ingram Spark.

Dedication

The book is dedicated to the brave people at Operation Underground Railroad who fight to end sex trafficking and modern-day slavery, supporting thousands of survivors in forty countries and all fifty US states.

www.ourrescue.org

Acknowledgments

To my amazing, talented, superstar editor, Stephanie Parent (USA), thank you, as always, for coming on this literary journey with me and for helping make these books the best they can be.

◆———◆

To my international club of beta readers who gave me their feedback, thank you. I truly value your thoughts.

In alphabetical order of first name:

Michele Kapugi, United States of America

Kim Schup, United States of America

Wayne Burnop, United States of America

✦⸺⸺✦

To all the kind and generous readers who take the time to review my novels and share their honest feedback, thank you so much. Your support is invaluable.

✦⸺⸺✦

I'm immensely grateful to you all for your kind and generous support, and would love to invite you for a glass of British Columbian wine or a cup of Ceylon tea with chocolates when you come to Vancouver next!

About the Author

T ikiri Herath is the multiple-award-winning author of international thriller and mystery novels and the Rebel Diva books.

❖—·—❖

Tikiri worked in risk management in the intelligence and defense sectors, including in the Canadian Federal Government and at NATO. She has a bachelor's degree from the University of Victoria, British Columbia, and a master's degree from the Solvay Business School in Brussels.

Born in Sri Lanka, Tikiri grew up in East Africa and has studied, worked, and lived in Europe, Southeast Asia, and North America throughout her adult life. An international nomad and fifth-culture kid, she now calls Canada home.

She's an adrenaline junkie who has rock climbed, bungee jumped, rode on the back of a motorcycle across Quebec, flown in an acrobatic airplane upside down, and parachuted solo.

When she's not plotting another thriller scene or planning another adrenaline-filled trip, you'll find her baking in her kitchen with a glass of red Shiraz in hand and vintage jazz playing in the background.

◆———◆

To say hello and get travel stories from around the world, go to www.Tikiriherath.com

Printed in Great Britain
by Amazon

27396041R00148